THE ROAN STALLION

The Legend of Big Heart · Book 2

Library of Congress Cataloging-in-Publication Data available upon request.

This is a work of historical fiction. All incidents, events, dialogue, names, and characters except for some well-known historical figures are products of the author's imagination and are not to be construed as real. Where real-life historical figures appear, the situations, incidents, and dialogues concerning those persons are fictional and are not intended to depict actual events. In all other respects, any likeness to actual persons, living or dead, or actual events is purely coincidental.

7th Generation
Book Publishing Company
PO Box 99
Summertown, TN 38483
888-260-8458
bookpubco.com
nativevoicesbooks.com

ISBN: 978-1-939053-48-0
E-book ISBN: 9781939053718

28 27 26 25 24 23   1 2 3 4 5 6 7 8 9

THE ROAN STALLION

The Legend of Big Heart · Book 2

Alfreda Beartrack-Algeo

7th GENERATION
Summertown, Tennessee

Contents

Thunder Rider

"Arrgh!" I moaned.

My left foot had caught in the door, and I'd landed on the porch floor with a thud. I was amazed at the size of the springs attached to every door on the farm. Even the shoddy outhouse had a fancy snapping spring. I guess Grandfather wanted to be sure none of the doors on the farm were left open. Maybe to keep the dust demons out.

I was in a hurry. I had grabbed a hot cookie from a tray where they were cooling, even though Mother had left a note saying, "Alfred, do not eat the cookies! They're for the community meeting tomorrow." I was trying to listen to the hushed voices coming from the back porch. I could smell the sage and cedar smoke, so I knew it was a serious conversation.

I thought I heard Mother mention to Grandmother something about my father, Elmer Swallow Sr. It had been two years since my father had to

leave our reservation to find work in the city.
He'd promised to come home after a year. I feared
he was dead, because he had broken his promise
to me.

I must be mistaken, I thought. Maybe they were
talking about my ten-year-old brother, Elmer Jr.

They must have heard me fall on the front
porch, because they quickly changed the subject.

"Has anyone seen my bread dough? I was
letting it rise on the back table," Mother called out.
"Elmer! Come and help me look for my dough.
I need to get my bread in the oven soon."

I was on my way to work at the Looking Rock
Ranch, southwest of Reliance, where I tamed wild
horses for the ranch owner. Even though I was
only thirteen years old, I'd always had a way with
horses, so he gave me the job. Reliance was a town
of about three hundred folks in southwest South
Dakota. The town had a railroad station for the
Chicago, Milwaukee, and Saint Paul railroad trains
that ran right through the town. It also had a bank,
a hardware store, several general stores, a school,
a newspaper, a trust and title office, a telegram
office, stagecoach and team transportation, and a
grain elevator.

My brother, Elmer, had planned to go with
me but changed his mind. He'd decided to stay
and help our mother and grandmother with their

cooking for tomorrow's big community meeting. Mainly, he would be fetching water and chopping wood for the cast-iron cookstove.

I grabbed my tack, saddle, and new birthday present, a colorful wool saddle blanket, and walked to the barn to saddle my horse, Anpo. Anpo, a brown-and-white paint mustang, was high-strung, intelligent, and a fast runner. Grandfather had just changed out his shoes, and I could tell from Anpo's whinny that he was eagerly waiting for me at his stall door.

I gave him a gentle knuckle-touch greeting. "Howdy, Po-Po Boy. Ready to ride?"

He nuzzled me with a soft nicker, letting me know he was ready to hit the trail.

I saddled up Anpo and led him to the shady side of the barn, where Grandfather was still shoeing horses. When Grandfather saw us approaching, he glanced up and smiled. His gray hair was neatly braided and wrapped in red cloth. Quite a contrast to the oil-soaked coveralls he was wearing. For as long as I could remember, Grandmother had combed, braided, and wrapped her husband's long hair in red cloth. She kept him handsomely groomed.

"Hi, Grandfather. I am leaving for Looking Rock Ranch and should be home before dark," I said.

Grandfather nodded without taking his eyes off the steel horseshoe he was nailing to one of our horse's hooves. "Be careful, Grandchild. Might get a storm later on today."

"I will, Grandfather," I answered.

My yellow Lab, Chepa, showed up with his pink tongue hanging out.

I grabbed him by his collar. "Come on, boy. It breaks my heart, but I have to tie you up so you don't follow me. A corral full of wild horses is not a safe place for you."

I tied him to the twisted juniper tree in the shade of the well house. I knew Elmer would keep an eye on him until I returned.

I rode past the main road south toward Beaver Creek. I was feeling good as I hummed a Lakota courtship song. I reached the fork in the road and decided to take a short detour to one of my favorite spots. I glanced up at the noonday sun; a white ball engulfed in a vast yellow hue blazed overhead. Even with the looks of the dark clouds building in the west, I had ample time to get to Looking Rock Ranch.

I untied the faded red bandana from around my neck and wiped the sweat from my eyes. Promising myself I wouldn't stay long, I turned left toward Beaver Creek. I coached Anpo toward the creek, but for some reason he resisted. I finally persuaded him it was okay as a golden eagle screeched above me. My medicine bundle, which hung from my neck, began throbbing. I knew the spirits were near, and I knew I was being watched over by my ancestors and my spirit helper, the golden eagle. But then a thought entered my mind. Maybe I was facing grave danger and my spirit helper knew I needed extra protection. I shook the thought off and continued on, despite a nagging sense of danger.

Dodging overhanging tree limbs in the dense woods, I found a good spot next to a spring and a large box elder tree. I was sure Anpo would be safe here, so I tied him to a limb and walked toward the nearby ridge for a better view. Quietly, I lay down in dried brown prairie grass with my rifle tucked under my arm. I had a good view of the creek when I saw him. *Hoka hey!*

A blue roan stallion grazed close to his herd of wild Nokota horses. The herd consisted of three small bands that stayed close to one another. They munched away under the watchful eye of the roan stallion.

I inched closer until I could see the roan stallion in better detail. His coat was magnificent. It had a blue gleam in the sunlight. His chest was deep, with a darker patch in the shape of a shield. His mane, tail, and all four legs up to the knees were a brilliant black. His face was lighter in color than the rest of his body, and a black patch covered the top of his head all the way down to his ears. It looked like he was wearing a black hat. He was a Medicine Hat horse, which was very sacred to my Lakota people. This was the first time I'd seen a Medicine Hat horse.

I thought perhaps the roan stallion and his Nokota herd were descendants of Chief Sitting Bull's legendary herd that was abandoned in these parts over forty years ago after Chief Sitting Bull's death.

The roan stopped grazing and raised his head to sniff the air. I thought, *Oh no, he picked up my scent.* But he went right back to munching the dried prairie grass. *Whew!* For a while, I worried surely he'd smelled my scent.

A crashing clap of thunder pulled my focus away from the roan stallion for just a second; the air was stifling, and not a blade of grass was moving. Something was coming.

An unfamiliar noise stunned me to my core. A high-pitched whistle rang out, matching the thunder rolling across the sky.

All of a sudden, a loud whinny echoed through the air! It was the roan stallion. He had picked up my scent. Thinking his herd was in danger, he was charging at me. Within seconds, the raging roan was in front of me. His ears were flattened, and he snorted and pawed the hard ground in warning. He was so close I could feel the hot air shooting from his flaring pink nostrils. I could see the whites of his eyes rolling wildly. For a second, my brown eyes locked with the roan stallion's blue eyes, and in an unexplainable moment, we were one and the same.

The moment passed when I spotted the funnel cloud in the distance headed straight toward us. I was shaking like a leaf in a twirling pile of autumn leaves. The air pressure was changing, and my ears started popping. I knew the roan felt it too by his squeals. The wind picked up with a deafening howl that was utterly terrifying. The storm hit us just as the roan stallion reared up, his powerful hooves aiming for my head. We were plucked up and sucked right into the bowels of the circular vortex of the tornado.

I prayed, *Great Spirit, Grandfather, please have mercy.*

The roan stallion and I rolled headfirst, over and over, higher and higher. I had to dodge his hooves and other debris coming from every direction. Soon, we were in the calm eye of the tornado, a small area colored with an uncanny yellow hue. The oxygen was getting thin, and I gasped for air. I cupped my hands over my mouth, trying to preserve what air I had. I glimpsed the roan floating next to me.

He was tossing his massive head from side to side, trying to breathe. A movement below caught my eye just as the ground started lifting up toward us. Suddenly, we were dropped into the deadly outer wall of the tornado's vortex. The force of the wind hitting the bottoms of my feet was excruciating. That roaring column wall swallowed me up and spit me right back out. I hit the ground in a ball of dust and debris. I was rolling and rolling over the prairie until everything went dark.

Team Time

The rain beating down on my face forced me to open my burning eyes. Slivers of blue light were breaking through the dark clouds above me. I slowly moved my legs and then my arms. Surprisingly, all parts seemed to be intact and working. I lifted my body up from the hard ground and slowly stood.

I was surprised I still had my new boots on my feet. Maybe it was a good thing that they were a little too tight, because they'd stayed on when it felt like everything was being sucked out of me. I had many cuts and bruises and a small gash above my left eye, but no broken bones or deep punctures. I was dazed but grateful. *Thank you, Creator.*

The tornado had lasted only a few minutes, although it felt like hours. From what I could figure, it dropped me about one-eighth of a mile northeast of Beaver Creek, where I'd left Anpo. In the distance, I could see the ridge where the roan stallion and I were picked up by the tornado.

My eyes spotted the roan stallion before I heard his squeals. He was entangled in a wire fence, and he was hurting and scared. Even though I was still shaken and not doing too good myself, I limped toward him. His blue eyes rolled up at me. He knew he was at my mercy.

After a careful assessment of the situation, I spotted a few areas where I could untwist the wire from where it was attached to the cedar corner fence post. I immediately went to work; I feared the roan stallion would go into shock any minute. My bleeding hands worked fast until the wires were untangled, ready to give way.

"Hotsy-totsy, we're good to go!" I said.

The roan stallion squealed loudly and brought himself up on all four legs, which were intact and held him up. Instead of running away like I expected, the roan stallion stood and faced me. My heart lodged in my throat. Once again, I was at his mercy. For a second time, our eyes locked. Within seconds, he bolted away into the darkness of the tree line, where I was sure his herd awaited his return.

I took off walking, and it seemed like I couldn't get back to the Beaver Creek fast enough. I prayed Anpo had survived the storm.

"Tweet," I whistled. "Come on, Anpo. Where are you, boy?" I hollered.

Finally, as I approached the creek, I heard the sweet sound of Anpo's whinny. Anpo stuck his long brown-and-white head out from behind the big tree I'd left him tied to. When he continued his whinny and moved his head up and down, I knew he was scolding me and welcoming me at the same time.

I patted his head. "Yes, I know. Once again, I didn't listen to my instincts and almost lost my life and yours too," I said.

I untied Anpo and mounted up. Although I was minus a good hat, I still had my mud-kickers on. I felt the nervous twitch of Anpo's muscles under me. I was sure he smelled the roan stallion's scent. Even he knew the roan was no ordinary horse.

My aching body dreaded the nine-mile ride to the Looking Rock Ranch. I dreaded getting tangled up with another ornery horse. I took the shortcut along a high ridge toward Medicine Butte. A quarter of a mile into our ride, a shadow fell across me and the surrounding ground. I jumped in my saddle, skittish from my ordeal.

Now what? I nervously looked up. It was only a flock of blackbirds flying overhead. Their high-pitched caw-caws didn't settle well with me for some reason. My medicine bundle vibrated against my chest under my storm-tattered shirt. I felt it was once again warning me of pending danger. I had a feeling of urgency to turn around and go back home. I knew something was drastically wrong at the farm. I was positive my boss, Mr. Looking Rock, would understand why I didn't show up at his ranch today. But for now, I needed to hightail it home. Fast!

I turned Anpo around. He was thrilled, since he knew the trail home by heart. The hour-long ride gave me a chance to think about my actions and maybe how to mend my foolish ways. But most of all, I had to have a good explanation to give Grandfather for not listening to him, even after I'd promised to go straight to the Looking Rock Ranch.

I could hear my mother now: "Alfred! You must learn to take advice and stop your irresponsible behavior. It is putting us all in jeopardy."

As hard as I tried to block them out, bits and pieces of memories came tumbling out of their own accord. I remembered when I was a skinny brown-skinned boy with big feet and long black braids, and my father was a big man with twinkling eyes and a broad smile. I remembered when Father would whisper ghostly horse secrets to me. He tried to teach me how to listen, to see, to feel, to taste, to smell, and to understand life, people, and especially a horse. But I was always defiant because I didn't like listening to grown-ups, especially my father.

When Father had to leave home to find work in the big city, he told me that he would love me as long as the stars filled the night sky, and he promised to be back soon. As he rode away, I cried and chased after him, but he just kept riding without looking back. Of all the bits and pieces, the memory of him not looking back stung the worst, like salt on my rope-burned hands.

It had been two years and two months since my father left to find work in the big city. He had not sent a letter, money, or anything. Everyone, including my mother, believed something terrible had happened and he was not returning home. Deep down, I thought my father was very disappointed in me and was probably much happier in the big city, far away from the farm and from me.

My mother, brother, and I had been living with my grandparents on their farm, in their log cabin, since my father left. Things had not been easy. Last fall, my grandfather downsized his livestock for several reasons. He was getting older, and it was harder to farm. It was hard to plant a field with his cows Sally and Sadie pulling the plow. The rainfall was getting less and less, and the crops were failing more and more. The markets had dropped into a recession, making the future of farming look bleak.

Grandfather held back a small herd of twenty cows, twelve horses, and six pigs, but Grandmother refused to give up any of her geese or chickens. In addition, the deer and elk were getting harder to find, and we had buffalo meat only on special occasions. At least for the stew pot, we had jack-rabbits galore.

Grandfather used to farm several fields of corn, wheat, and oats, which he sold for income. This year was definitely different. He had not planted wheat and would be keeping most of his corn and oats for livestock feed. He reassured me that everything was fine, but I didn't believe him.

Grandfather needed a gas-powered tractor to make his work much easier, and I aimed to get him one. Mr. Looking Rock's neighbor, Mark Schneider, had a tractor for sale for three hundred and fifty dollars. It was a lot of money, but I had a secret plan.

With my horse, Anpo, and Blake, my friend Orson's horse, I planned on winning the five-hundred-dollar prize money at the upcoming relay race at the White River Frontier Days on August 2. The pair would make a good relay team, since both horses were fast, high-spirited, and dependable enough to win any race. The prize money would be enough to buy Mark Schneider's tractor. I knew my friend Orson would not hesitate to help me. He was spending time in Rosebud with his uncle Ralph but would be coming home next week.

There was only one problem: I needed another horse for the relay team. I knew of one horse that could help win the prize money: the blue roan stallion. I had to find him and a way to gain his trust. I was sure I could find a way.

I reached the bluffs overlooking the Iron Nation community and saw the Messiah Episcopal Church, the schoolhouse, and a few scattered houses. Next, I saw my grandparents' cabin and their red granary. *Whew!* Iron Nation had survived the storm.

I rode directly to the barn and water trough. I left Anpo saddled up. He was happy to be home and splashed water everywhere with his lips and muzzle. I ran toward the cabin, anxious to make sure everyone was okay. Elmer met me at the back door. I immediately knew something was drastically wrong by the dried tears on his face.

"Chepa's dead!" Elmer cried.

Second Chance

o! Chepa can't be dead! You probably made a mistake! Where is he?" I shouted. I'd either misunderstood my brother or was unwilling to believe him. "How? What happened?"

"Over there." Elmer pointed toward the juniper tree where I'd left Chepa tied up that morning. His shaky voice rambled on. "I went to play ball with him after you left for the ranch, and he wasn't moving. His head was at an odd angle in a puddle of thick milky foam. I prayed you'd come home. Alfred, what are we going to do?"

"I don't know," I answered.

I pressed on Chepa's stomach, and a foul-smelling liquid frothed from his mouth. I pressed my hand against his neck, but I couldn't feel a pulse. I opened his mouth, looking for an obvious obstruction, but his airway was clear. I just couldn't understand what had happened. Maybe

17

he'd eaten a poisonous plant or mushrooms. In any case, Chepa was surely dead.

As much as I tried to be strong, I broke down sobbing. *My best friend has left me forever.* I held his lifeless body and rocked him back and forth.

Grandfather touched my shoulder. "I am so sorry for your loss, Grandson. For our loss. He was a good dog. The best ever. We will miss him. The spirits let me know you were trapped in the storm. I prayed the thunder beings would be merciful to you and spare your life. I had no idea they would take Chepa's."

He handed me a small bag of tobacco and sage. "Better get him buried, Grandson. As hot as it is, he won't keep long in this heat."

I looked up at Grandfather. "I am going to bury him at our favorite place, near the hollowed-out cottonwood tree at Medicine Creek."

He nodded and gently patted my shoulder. We hoisted Chepa's eighty-pound lifeless body over the back of Anpo. We tied him securely with a rope, along with a shovel for digging a grave. Carrying the medicine bag, I led Chepa on his last big adventure to Medicine Creek.

I could never forget the day I found him alone in the middle of the road: It was on a Saturday and my birthday, May 24, 1923. I was so happy to turn six years old. I was riding with my father with his prized team hitched to the wagon. We were headed for supplies at the hardware store in Reliance. My father always made me feel extra special when we did things together, especially on my birthday. I knew he would let me buy a box of Cracker Jack, a sweet mixture of popcorn and peanuts with a tiny surprise inside. I squirmed in the wagon seat with excitement. I could hardly wait.

We were almost to Main Street when I saw something in the middle of the road. I shouted over the click-clack of the horses. "Father, look up ahead! It's a dog! Please stop!"

We stopped and climbed down from the wagon to get a look at the pup. I couldn't explain it, but it felt like that little helpless pup was waiting for me. He was alone and hungry. His four oversized, dust-caked feet were attached to the ends of four shaking, skinny legs. We couldn't see the color of his fur because of the layers of mud, cockleburs, and dried tumbleweeds stuck to him.

He was starving, but still, his little tail was wagging, and his pink tongue greeted us with a lick. Father pulled his sweat-stained bandana off his neck and wiped the dust off the pup's front legs, uncovering streaks of yellow fur.

"It's a little male yellow Labrador. I'll be dog-gone," said Father.

I said, "Maybe he's just lost and somebody is looking for him."

Father lifted the skinny yellow pup into the back of the wagon and said, "Maybe someone at the feedstore will recognize him."

We asked at the hardware store and around town if anyone had lost a Labrador pup, but no one knew a thing or even seemed to care.

We headed back to Iron Nation loaded up with feed, groceries, supplies, and a little yellow pup. I named him Chepa. He'd grow fast into his big feet and would become my constant companion.

I found the place. It was a small clearing hidden by shoulder-to-shoulder trees. In the middle of the clearing was a mighty cottonwood tree with her arms arched toward the heavens and her roots twisted deep into the earth.

Dreading the task ahead, I clenched my teeth and grabbed the shovel. I was determined to see this through. I announced my intentions to Mother Earth to get her permission and blessings to dig into her.

I started digging, and it didn't take long to break through the hard ground. Soon, I had a knee-high pile of fresh dirt and a hole dug deep enough to keep my friend safe from scavengers. I felt something watching me, and a chill creeped down the back of my neck. A low growl followed by a high-pitched scream came from the dense woods nearby.

It was old Ned, the lone cougar who had been roaming around these parts for as long as I could remember. Ned was missing teeth and a few claws; he was pretty much harmless. Most locals avoided him and just let him be. I figured it was good to let him hang around because he kept the timber wolves at bay. Chepa never had much interest in old Ned but tolerated him. Perhaps he came to pay one last visit to Chepa. My father taught me that animals have a sense about things like that.

I slid Chepa's body off Anpo's back next to his grave. He fell to the ground with a thud. White foam had dried around his mouth.

I offered my prayer: *Great Spirit, thank you for blessing the last seven years with such a good dog and loyal friend.* I sprinkled a pinch of traditional tobacco inside the grave. I sang a Lakota warrior song for Chepa's journey home to the spirit world.

I brushed Chepa down with sage and slid his body toward the deep grave. I stopped in my tracks and watched the foam start bubbling from his mouth again. I dropped to my knees next to Chepa's body and felt for a pulse. I gasped and jumped back in surprise. *Whooooaaa.*

Chepa opened a bloodshot eye. When he saw me, he started wagging his tail. *Great holy ones, what is this? Has his ghost come back for me?*

I couldn't believe it! Chepa was alive? Whatever he'd eaten was wearing off. But I knew I had to act fast. I dragged him to the top of the dirt pile and turned him around until his head was lower than his body. I alternated between shaking him and massaging his stomach. Globs of yeast gurgled out of his mouth. Soon, a considerable pile of reeking fermented dough was heaped up on the ground below Chepa's head.

Everything hit at once. Of course! It was Chepa who'd stolen Mother's missing yeast dough from the back porch that morning. He'd eaten it all and was in a drunken coma all day.

Chepa jumped up and sheepishly licked my hand. He seemed to sense he'd done something wrong that almost cost him his life. I was so relieved, I didn't have the heart to scold him.

Instead, I hugged him close. "Chepa, you gave me quite a scare. You're a very lucky dog. Most dogs do not survive eating dough, but you did. I'm so happy that you are alive. Come on! Let's fill this hole and get back home. We need to let the family know the good news."

Chepa was thirsty and hungry and in a wild frenzy to get home. Anpo and I could barely keep up with him. I thought, *Who would have known Chepa would die and come back to life? My friend Orson sure won't believe this one.*

It was a day out of the ordinary, for sure. And I was sure Mr. Looking Rock would understand why I hadn't shown up for work today. I would deal with that on Monday. Today, I wanted to rejoice over a reunion with my best friend. Chepa darted off the trail when he spotted his dinner, a jackrabbit, running across the field.

Medicine Hat

y family was crowded together on the front yard, with mouths dropped open in surprise. I was sure we made quite the spectacle: my face flushed with excitement, Anpo stepping high and frisky, and Chepa trotting with a small jackrabbit in his mouth.

Elmer was the most flabbergasted. He ran toward us and threw his arms around Chepa's neck. "Chepa! Are you for real? Are you really alive?"

Chepa shoved his nose against Elmer, letting him know he was alive.

With a twinkle in his eye, Grandfather said, "Howdy! Look at this!"

That evening, I told Chepa's story over and over. I added a little more flair each time. The more I told Chepa's story, the harder we laughed.

Grandmother said in her wise voice, "When a living being is believed dead and comes back to life, the Great Spirit adds years back onto that living creature's life span. Let's count on Chepa being around a long time."

It was a hot and sultry night. After my family tired of hearing Chepa's story, Grandmother said, "It's too hot inside the cabin. I think we need to sleep on the screened-in front porch."

We all agreed. Elmer and Mother made a bed on the floor of the porch at one end, and Chepa and I were at the other end. Grandfather had an old army cot he kept on the porch for nights like this. Since Grandmother was our family matriarch, she slept on the comfortable willow couch. Everyone settled in for the night except Grandfather and me. We sat up and talked. I felt the time was right to share my story with my grandfather.

"Grandfather, I had an encounter with an unusual roan horse earlier today on my way to the Looking Rock Ranch," I said.

Grandfather cleared his throat.

I continued, "Grandfather, I encountered a Medicine Hat roan stallion today."

This caught his attention, and he sat straight up.

I said, "I know I promised you this morning that I'd go straight to the ranch, and I didn't. I'm sorry for that. I've been watching a herd of wild Nokota horses roaming near Medicine Creek for the past two weeks, especially the roan stallion."

The wind blew the flame of the kerosene lamp out. Grandfather said, "Keep talking, Grandson. It's okay."

I continued on, "You should see him. He is stunning. His coat is a brilliant indigo blue with a lighter-hued face. Four black feet up to the hocks, and a flowing black mane and tail. The strangest thing is the black patch covering his ears and the entire top of the head. It looks just like he's wearing a hat. He also has an unusual black mark on his chest that is shaped just like a shield. But most impressive, Grandfather, is his intense sky-blue eyes. It felt like he was looking deep inside of me."

Sucking in my breath, I said, "The roan stallion charged me, and we were picked up by a tornado in the middle of his attack. By some miracle, the tornado dropped us close to the ground. I found the roan stallion tangled up in a wire fence, so I freed him. It was odd, because I wasn't afraid of him. I believe the sky spirit brought us together for a reason."

Grandfather replied, "A roan horse is a sight to behold. They are not really blue. Their coats have an even mixture of black and white hairs that appears blue. Now, the roan stallion being a Medicine Hat horse makes him more special."

"Why is that, Grandfather?" I asked.

Grandfather answered, "A Medicine Hat horse is very rare and very holy. Our Lakota people believe they have supernatural ability to protect their riders from injury, harm, and even death during a battle."

He sighed. "Only once in my life have I seen a Medicine Hat horse. It was 1882, and I was twenty-two years old. I was granted a pass from our Indian agent to leave my Sicangu, Burnt Thigh, reservation. This was a time when South and North Dakota were one territory. I was helping round up a wild horse herd for the government, to be shipped to Omaha, Nebraska. We were camped next to a Hunkpapa camp on the Standing Rock Sioux Reservation.

"We had the wild herd contained in a make-shift corral when one of the cowboys saw a lone Medicine Hat roan stallion standing on a hill watching us. Chief Sitting Bull's herd of Nokota horses was grazing not far from our camp. No one knew where the stallion came from, but he was not afraid. He walked into camp and up to Chief Sitting Bull's lodge.

"We honored the roan stallion's presence with a horse dance ceremony. Only our Chief, Sitting Bull, was allowed to ride him. He kept him as one of his horses and a stallion for his Nokota herd.

"I have never seen a horse such as the blue roan again," Grandfather said. "Grandson, you must load your sacred pipe and go to your elder, Pete Flying Crow, to help you interpret your encounter with the sky spirit and with the sacred Medicine Hat horse. There is a deeper meaning here, and he has the gift to know what that is. Meanwhile, you must listen to me and stop taking dangerous risks."

I nodded, all the while dreading the thought of visiting Grandfather Pete Flying Crow. He never forgot anything, especially my pending vision quest.

"Good night, Grandson," Grandfather said.

"Good night, Grandfather," I replied.

Ranch Ties

The week quickly passed. Mr. Looking Rock was very understanding when I explained why I missed a day of work. I shared Chepa's story with him, but I wasn't ready to tell him about the wild roan stallion. He might have thought that my idea to tame the roan and build a relay team was silly. I was worried he might try and discourage me or, worse yet, tell my grandfather.

I thought I was making progress with the roan stallion. I was trying to get him to trust me, so I left him sugar cubes and dried apples. I was hoping to make physical contact with the roan stallion again soon.

Tomorrow was branding day at the ranch, a big event in this territory. We were scheduled to start around daybreak, so I decided to ride to the ranch that afternoon and spend the night in the bunkhouse. I wanted to be ready to get to work bright and early.

Riding along, I thought about Mr. Karl Looking Rock. His father was Sicangu Lakota from Rosebud Agency, and his mother was the daughter of a German homesteader. Mr. Looking Rock was a short, stocky man in his late forties, with a heart of gold. He had taken me under his wing to teach me everything he knew about horses, and I appreciated it greatly.

I could tell Mr. Looking Rock was very lonely. He'd lost his wife two days after she gave birth to their only child, James. James died a year later from influenza, and Mr. Looking Rock never remarried. He'd lost his family, and in my heart, I'd lost my father. We both had holes in our hearts, and together we made a whole unbroken heart.

After unloading my gear in the bunkhouse, I decided to walk toward the main house and find Mr. Looking Rock. There he was, in the front yard. He was leaning up against a new red Chevy one-ton grain truck, talking to a young man. The resemblance between the two men was striking. Same height and build, thick dark brown hair, and close-set eyes, with a long nose and flared nostrils. I was sure there was a blood connection.

Mr. Looking Rock saw me and called me over. "Alfred, my son, I want you to meet my nephew, Johnny Krugerbery. Johnny is my late sister-in-law Hanna's son. He just moved here from Denver. He will be staying in the extra bunkhouse until he can get himself a sturdy cabin built."

He said to Johnny, "I have taken Alfred as my son. He practically lives here at the ranch. I'm sure you'll get used to seeing him around." Mr. Looking Rock turned to me. "Alfred, I know you've been addressing me as Mr. Looking Rock out of respect, but please, I would like you to call me Karl. It is more personal."

I nodded. "I like that, Mr. Looking Rock, ummm, I mean Karl." I smiled big and extended a hardy handshake toward Johnny. "I am glad to meet you, Johnny. I had no idea Mr. Looking Rock had relatives in the big city."

Johnny refused to shake my hand.

Mr. Looking Rock didn't notice the snobbery, or maybe he didn't want to notice. For whatever reason, Johnny Krugerbery thought I was a threat. I knew I had an enemy at the Looking Rock Ranch. My medicine rock moved against my skin. I would have to be extra careful.

Tomorrow was my first big roundup, and I could hardly wait. That evening, though, I enjoyed sitting with Karl and two of his hired hands, sipping coffee. It felt good being with other people who loved horses just as much as I did. I could tell by the intensity of their voices and laughter that the coffee they were drinking was different from what I was drinking. I was enjoying the serenade from a chorus of crickets and the relaxed laughter of Karl and his hired hands. Johnny Krugerbery was nowhere to be seen, but I wasn't too upset over that at all.

Unable to tame my curiosity, I asked, "Karl, how did you and your family end up ranching in the Dakotas?"

He said, "My mother was Lydia Krugerbery. Her father was Justus Krugerbery, and her mother was Leonie Kraus Krugerbery. They came to this country from the Volga steppe region in Russia. They had originally moved to the Volga region from Germany. A man visited their community one day and told them of a place where land was free and dreams became reality. A short time later, my grandparents moved here to Dakota Territory and filed a claim for a homestead. That homestead is now the Looking Rock Ranch.

"My grandparents had no idea their new land had been forcefully taken from the Great Sioux Nation. This didn't sit too well with my grandparents. They became good allies of the Lakota people in the region. My grandparents had three daughters: Claudia, Hanna, and my mother, Lydia.

"My father, Bruce Looking Rock, was from the Rosebud Lakota Sioux Agency, not too far from here. His father was Harold Looking Rock. My grandfather Harold managed a trading post on the reservation, and my father, Bruce, helped out in his store a lot. My mother met my father while visiting the trading post, and it was love at first sight. Not long after they met, they married against the wishes of my mother's family and moved here to this ranch. My parents had three sons, Abe, David, and myself. Abe and David are gone. It's just me now."

Karl let out a deep sigh. "Young man, it's best you turn in for the night. Tomorrow will be long and hard and here before you know it."

He was right. Carrying a small kerosene lamp to light the path, I walked to the smaller bunkhouse for some shut-eye. I liked the feeling of my new leather chaps rubbing against my legs. It reminded me I was in the big league now. Unrolling my bedroll, I threw it on the top bunk.

Just when I was crawling under the scratchy wool blanket, I was yanked up by my hair. It was Johnny Krugerbery. He held me by the hair against the bunkhouse wall. With a thick German accent, he said, "Don't think you're pulling the wool over my eyes, you fool! Tryin' to take advantage of my uncle to get at his dough. I know your kind. All you Injuns, nothing but no-good savages. You just stay clear away from me, ya hear, kid?"

Trembly, I nodded in agreement.

Johnny Krugerbery gave me one last push toward the floor. As he left the bunkhouse, he muttered, "Darn kid is messing up my plans. Will have to teach him a lesson."

Touching my medicine bundle, I held it and prayed for protection from Johnny Krugerbery. I thought about my father. I missed him the most in times like these.

It didn't take long to drift off to sleep. A familiar hand pulled me into a dream world where I was riding the roan stallion. We galloped effortlessly across the heavens. Far above were rolling clouds of gray and blue. A thunderbird flew at us from the clouds, his eyes shooting electric lightning bolts. One of the bolts struck me in the heart. I held tight to the medicine roan stallion, but he was struck too. We tumbled together into a dark tunnel.

Big Day

 voice startled me out of my deep slumber. It was Butch, one of the hired hands. "Come on, get up, boy! It's four thirty and about time you woke up. Big day ahead."

I couldn't believe it. Seemed like I had just closed my eyes, and now it was already morning. The smell of coffee and bacon filled the air. First order of business was making my way to the outhouse. When I stumbled back to the bunkhouse, I found the washbasin and splashed my face with cold water. *Whew!* That woke me up good.

Walking toward the main house for breakfast, I couldn't shake off the spirit dream from the previous night. I knew one thing for certain: the roan stallion and I had a destiny together. Maybe even winning a relay race. After finishing my breakfast, I went to find Anpo to feed him and get him saddled. It was his first big roundup too.

Anpo was very happy to see me. I gently rubbed him down and reassured him.

"It's going to be fine, boy. Let's get you fed and saddled up. We have a long day ahead of us."

Leaning on him, I let him feel my heart. I let him know I wasn't going anywhere. His trembling eased, and his muzzle nudged me hard, telling me he was hungry—now!

We were both ready for our big adventure. Instead of keeping his horses in stalls, Karl allowed his horses to graze in fenced pastures along the freshwater creek. He fed them high-quality grain on a regular feeding schedule. His horses ate much better than Anpo.

Several experienced cowboys from neighboring ranches were starting to show up to help with the branding. Marc Thunder, another hired hand, divided us into teams. I was riding with four other riders: Cheyenne, Jacob, Bird Man, and Jack.

We rounded up the horses and brought them into the barn area and corrals. Marc separated the foals from the mares, and I herded the foals into separate pens. The stubborn ones we lured in with sweet oats.

Bird Man was guiding the yearlings into holding pens on the north end of the barnyard. Cheyenne was bringing the colts and fillies into holding pens on the east side, and Jacob was working the geldings into the smaller pastures. Since Jack was the most experienced, he was the only one corralling the stallions.

I was having difficulty hearing the other men over the piercing whinnies of the younger horses. I had to depend on body language and hand signs to communicate with the other riders. The older horses also felt the stress of the moment and ran in circles. In my opinion, it was a mess. But the other men seemed to take it in stride.

I noticed the branding irons all had the same brand, Bar-K-Bar. I assumed that was Karl's registered family brand. Cheyenne buried the branding irons in a glowing bed of coals and quickly pulled them out when they turned an ashen color. He barely touched the hot iron to the rear of the horse for a second. By the time the horse knew what was happening, he was sporting a Bar-K-Bar brand. The brand was permanent and turned the hair that grew back a different color.

I looked over at Karl. He was separating his best thoroughbred male horses from the mix. They would become his breeding stallions. After the branding ordeal, all the horses were given vaccinations and dental and hoof examinations. The horses that needed them were given a new set of shoes. During the day, I caught Johnny Krugerbery staring at me twice. I made it a point to avoid him like a plague.

Buffalo feathers! I was exhausted, and it was only high noon. We broke for lunch in shifts to eat and take care of our horses. When it was my shift, I first went to check on Anpo. I was holding him in the very last pen near the wooded area along Big Cat Creek, because it had more shade. He didn't like all the unfamiliar frenzy one tad. After feeding and watering him, I rubbed him down with my hands. He always liked that. It didn't take long before he was nuzzling me in return.

Walking back to the branding area, I noticed a movement far to the south in the shadows of the creek. I stopped to look. *Whoa!* I thought I could make out the roan stallion. He was standing perfectly still, watching me. Maybe he was roused by the cries of the mares. Or maybe he'd had the same dream I had, and he'd come looking for me. Either way, it made my day to see him there.

A loud shout from Bird Man snapped me out of my thoughts.

"Alfred, look out! The horses are right upon you. Quick! Open the gate! Now!"

I quickly pried open the wooden gate. It swung back and hit the cedar railing just in time. Three charging and excited mares were running toward me. I shooed them right into the holding pen.

"Whew, that was a close call," I shouted at Bird Man.

Pulling my leather gloves off, I removed my cotton bandana from around my head. It was a good feeling to let the wind air-dry the salty sweat beads running down my forehead.

Again, I heard Bird Man shouting like a wild man. "Hey, someone catch that bay gelding. He needs to be dewormed and vaccinated."

I stopped the gelding with my lasso and gently led him toward the pen. I whispered in his ear. "It's okay, boy, don't be frightened. You'll be eating a nice mouthful of pasture grass real soon."

I gave him a knuckle touch, and he immediately calmed down. He didn't have a problem at all letting Bird Man inspect him.

The delicious aroma of grilled steaks and mountain oysters let me know it was time to round down the roundup. I joined Bird Man, Cheyenne, Jacob, and Jack at the far holding pens.

Watching the baby foals' happy reunion with their mothers made me smile. When the mares found their babies, they reared up on their front legs and neighed loudly. The baby foals, in turn, tried to mimic their mothers by rearing up and giving a squeaky neigh. Unable to keep their balance, they were falling backward on the grassy pasture.

Back at the main house, we all agreed it was a successful day. Worth the blood, sweat, and exhaustion. I decided to spend another night. I knew Anpo would not like my decision one bit. I would think of something special to make it up to him. If I stayed another night, maybe I could find out what Johnny Krugerbery was really up to and why he'd come to live at Looking Rock Ranch.

A Soldier's Demise

everal weeks had passed since I started training the roan stallion. Progress was better than I expected. Hoping to get a jumpstart on my chores so I could get to the roan, I started irrigating the fields earlier than usual. Dawn broke in an array of pink and lavender that streaked across the eastern sky. I offered my tobacco and welcomed the new day.

Within minutes, the sun danced his warmth across the land. I thought, *Howdy, another sultry, rainless day*. Chepa playfully romped through the rows of tender cornstalks, sending a flock of angry blackbirds skyward.

I said, "Whoa . . . slow down, Cheep! We don't want to cause any damage. Chepa, look over yonder. There's a nice fat rabbit waiting just for you."

Chepa spotted the cottontail and sped off across the field lickety-split, in hot pursuit. I thought,

Good, the rabbit chase will keep him occupied for a while.

The fenced-in cornfield was in an ideal location. It was nestled next to Medicine Creek and protected on two sides by rugged bluffs. I opened up the last irrigation pipe, and the water ran down the corn furrows and spilled into the adjoining oat field. I was thrilled at how tall our corn plants were and also surprised they'd survived the last two hailstorms. With the increasing dry winds, dust storms, and grasshoppers, crop survival was day by day.

I looked across the fertile fields and thought about the fire that had licked across this land last summer. The fire was started by Superintendent O'Neil, a corrupt man who'd tried to push my grandfather and our family off our land. My grandfather met every attack with a prayer.

One good thing that came from the fire was that the land benefited from the charcoal left behind. The soil was enhanced with nitrogen and numerous nutrients, everything needed to grow outstanding corn and oat crops.

I hit my faded denim trousers with a good drumbeat. My prayer rose in song to the sky and earth. *SLAP . . . slap . . . SLAP . . . slap . . .*

"Cloud maiden soft and full—scoots across a beautiful sky . . . hey-ya-ho . . .

Corn maiden tall and tender—her stalks so green and high . . . hey-ya-ho . . .

Up and high she goes—as high as a buffalo eye . . . hey-ya-ho . . .

Right past the trees—toward cloud maiden in the sky . . . hey-ya-ho-Hey."

I decided I would return to check on the fields this evening. For now, I needed to get back to the farm to water the garden and feed the animals. Chepa followed, eager for some action. I was geared up and ready to work with the roan at Beaver Creek.

"Son, do you have a minute? I want to talk with you." My mother's head popped out from between two dust-stained sheets that whipped in the hot summer breeze.

I said, "Sure, Mother."

She pinned the last shirt up with two wooden clothespins and turned to me and said, "Just trying to get the laundry dried before any afternoon dust storms should happen to roll in. Seems like they are happening more and more these days."

I joined her at the wooden table under the sprawling willow that provided shade for most of the backyard. My mother's small brown hands clenched her worn, faded apron until her knuckles turned white. Her set jaw contrasted with the curves of her beautiful, kind face. It was the look of determination.

With bated breath, I waited for her words. I tried to think of things she was going to say to me.

My mother said, "Do you remember me telling you that our Lower Brule Agency moved its headquarters to Crow Creek Agency in Fort Thompson at the beginning of this year?"

I nodded. "Yes, I do."

She continued, "A telegram was sent to Superintendent Wright's office. The telegram was from Mr. Burt Holiday from Battle Mountain Sanitarium in Hot Springs."

Tears spilled out from the corners of her eyes. They trickled down her cheekbones and dropped onto her white knuckles.

After a deep breath, my mother continued, "Son, your father is alive. But he is gravely ill."

Her words felt like a punch in my solar plexus. I didn't recognize the high, wobbly voice that came out of my mouth. "How? What? My father? I don't understand."

My mother patted my tightly scrunched shoulders. "Are you all right, Son? Do you want me to continue?"

I mumbled, "Yes, please do, Mother."

My mother said, "Your father was involved in a mining accident at Homestake Mine in Lead, South Dakota, over a year ago. He was one of seven men trapped in the mine. He was the lone survivor. After the mining accident, your father was transported by a mule team through the hills to Battle Mountain Sanitarium in Hot Springs."

I asked, "Why Battle Mountain Sanit . . . er . . . een, or whatever it's called?"

She said, "Battle Mountain Sanitarium is a special hospital for soldiers. Because your father is a highly decorated soldier, with a Distinguished Service Order Medal, he was provided care at the hospital."

I asked, "Why have we just now found all this out? Why didn't the hospital let us know sooner?"

My mother said, "Several telegrams were sent to our agency last year, but ex-superintendent O'Neil destroyed each one. But now we know. That's all that matters."

Holding my shoulders square, my mother looked me in the eyes. "Alfred, my son, your father is fighting for his life. I must go to him as soon as possible. I must depend on you now, more than ever. Please keep a watchful eye on Elmer. He's been hanging out with the mischievous Bull Elk twins. I don't want him at the river unattended."

I croaked out my words: "Yes, Mother, don't worry. You can count on me."

I understood her heart. This could be the last time my mother would see my father alive.

I locked Chepa in the barn, knowing Elmer would let him out later on. I didn't want him to follow me. I was hesitant about leaving my mother and family in such a state, but I wanted to get to the roan stallion. I led Anpo toward the main road, still undecided. I didn't see my grandfather silently standing in the shadow of the front gate. When he moved, I about jumped ten feet in the air.

Grandfather motioned toward Beaver Creek with his chin. "Looks like you're mighty excited to get to that roan stallion."

I answered, "Yes, I am, but I feel like I should stay home today. Mother just shared with me the news about my father, and I don't feel very good right now."

My grandfather knew me better than anyone else. He knew how I disliked unexpected news or events. I was sure he knew how devastating the news about my father was to me.

I decided to tell him my plans for the relay horse race.

"I have been working hard to tame the blue roan. He's going to be part of my relay team for the upcoming White River Frontier Days. Mr. Karl Looking Rock has decided to sponsor us. He will also pay our entrance fee and help transport our horses to White River."

Grandfather said, "That's great news, Grandson. I will share this news with your grandmother. She might want to camp at the White River fair. We used to camp there every year for many years. I can't remember why we stopped. I'm sure if any horse could win a race for you, it would be a roan stallion. Our horses are sacred, and so are our horse relay races. They remind us of the old days, of our warrior traditions, and of our buffalo. But please be careful. Remember, you're dealing with a high-strung wild stallion, and a Medicine Hat on top of that."

I could agree to be careful, but I couldn't agree to go slow. Time was short if I wanted to win a relay race and buy him a tractor.

Because my spirit felt like I needed to stay home, I turned Anpo around and led him back to the barn. I unsaddled Anpo and decided to keep him in the small pasture for the night. That way, I wouldn't have to chase him down tomorrow when I was ready to leave for Beaver Creek.

The day passed quickly, and night came just as fast. It felt very nice to spend time with my family. Grandfather led us in prayer over the supper meal and fanned everyone with cedar smoke. He asked the Great Spirit to heal my father and bring him home to us.

I went to my bedroom early because I wanted to work on a painting I was designing. The night was sultry, and my room was hot. I opened my window, hoping I might catch a small breeze. I didn't. The only thing that came through was the cries of coyotes calling to one another in the night.

Trust or Bust

When I fell into a deep sleep, I could see a dot of light coming toward me. It grew bigger and bigger until the roan stallion stood in front of me. Effortlessly I slipped upon his back and grabbed his mane. We flew to a place where the tails of shooting stars were like memories unbroken. I awoke long enough to watch, through my open window, a shooting star race across the night sky. I felt a calm peace inside. I drifted back into the darkness of sleep.

Morning arrived much too fast. I went through the motions of daily chores, but my mind was on the roan. When it was finally quitting time, Anpo and I rode south toward Beaver Creek. It was too dangerous for a dog to wander around at Beaver Creek. I usually left Chepa behind when I worked with the roan, even though it about broke his heart.

The roan showed promise once we developed some trust between us. I was convinced the roan had been domesticated and trained at some point. But I sensed a dark pain in his spirit. A pain as calloused as the welt scars on his rump. Perhaps something, or someone, hurt him badly, and trust was a key issue.

I tied Anpo along the creek bottom. As long as he had plenty of water, shade, and dry brown grass to eat, he didn't mind being tied up. I reached the small hill above the creek bottom. I whistled for the roan. It didn't take long, and the roan was in front of me. I clucked my tongue against the roof of my mouth. He recognized the sound and knew he had a treat coming.

The roan didn't hesitate to curl his lips around the apple and finished it off in two bites. I knew the roan and the other wild horses were used to eating wild grasses, so I avoided giving him anything too rich or overdoing the treats.

The roan loved being brushed down and pampered. Upon close inspection of the roan's teeth, I could see dark indentations in the center of his grinding teeth. I assumed he was between four and five years old. He was the perfect age for high-endurance racing.

It was time. I held a rope halter in my left hand and another apple in the other.

I sweet-talked the roan: "It's okay, Blue Wonder of Wonders. I'm not going to hurt you."

I held my hand near his ear and gently slipped the rope halter around his neck. I tied a lead rope to it. The roan reared up, but I kept my foot on the end of the rope.

"You have to trust me," I coaxed.

He tried to rear up again and buck. I applied more pressure to the rope and gently pulled his head to the ground. I used verbal cues and walked him in wide circles. The roan adjusted to the situation far better than I expected. He seemed very familiar with a lead rope. I was totally convinced that sometime in his mysterious past, he had been trained. I was thrilled with how everything was falling into place.

It was time to test the roan's trust. I approached him on his left side. I leaned my full body weight against him. The roan twitched and snorted, but he stood still.

My father's leather hackamore, a bitless bridle, rested on my forearm. I gently slipped the reins over the roan's head. I waited a minute before I removed the halter. He was bridled up, and I was gung ho to make my dream come true.

I decided to springboard from a standing position. I held the reins snugly, and I swung my leg over the roan's bare back. He felt the weight of my body on his back for the first time. He danced to one side and buck-jumped to the other. I held on. It was vicious for a few seconds. *Whew!* I was sweating bullets.

I molded my body to the roan. He felt my rhythm and my balance, and I felt his. A couple of times he tried to put his head down, ready to buck. I pulled back on the reins, just enough to gain leverage.

I said, "Okay, Wonderous One, we're in this together. Let's get it on!"

I urged him on with my legs, knees, hands, and seat. As he picked up speed, my long, loose black hair tangled in the wind with his black mane. We rode fearlessly together. The roan found his rhythm and kept a steady gait. His body was warm under me.

"Screeeech! Screeeech!" A golden eagle swooped overhead. I felt exuberant emotions through my entire being. I was free.

Not wanting to wear his trust thin, I decided to end our riding adventure. The roan snorted and danced. He'd enjoyed the ride as much as I had.

"We did it, boy. Now, to get you to stand still."

I held the reins with both hands, leaned forward, and swung my leg over the roan's back. Both of my feet hit the ground. I felt like I was still moving.

After cooling the roan down, I removed the leather hackamore from him. I gave him a good pat. "Get back to your herd. Your mares are waiting for you."

Anpo was in good sorts, given he was tied to a sprawling cottonwood. I had one apple left, and he made short work of it.

On the way home, I took a look at the smaller south pasture above my grandparents' farm for a spot to build a training area. I walked in circles and measured the area with my feet.

I mumbled to myself, "Yes! This will work. It's level, with very little brush and rocks to clear. The clay soil is perfect for good drainage. It will do just fine. I will ask my grandfather to use his plow and to clear rocks and level the ground."

I reached the main road around midafternoon. I noticed a distorted mirage ahead. It blurred in and out in the dancing heat waves. I wiped my sweat-caked eyes so I could get a better look.

I said to myself, "Whoa . . . No way!"

The swagger instantly gave him away. It was my next best friend, Orson, since Chepa was my first best friend. He was walking down the middle of the road like he owned it. He walked in the direction of my grandparents' farm.

I muttered to myself, "Well, this is as cool as snake's hips."

When we got to the road's hard surface, the ping of Anpo's new shoes was hard to miss. We were right behind Orson—*clip-clop, clip-clop, clip-clop, clip-clop*—but he pretended not to hear us. He continued on without looking back.

"Hoka! Move over, greenhorn, unless you want to get trampled under!" I shouted.

Orson spun around. Grabbing my leg, he pulled me right off Anpo. He wrestled me down and tried desperately to twist my arm behind my back. He couldn't pin me. We grunted like two territorial bucks, neither one willing to give in. Finally, I hog-tied him.

We stood up and brushed ourselves off.

Orson said, "Holy moley, my friend, you grew some muscles since I last saw you."

I answered, "Yeppers! I just proved it to you."

We walked the remaining quarter mile home in friendly conversation. Anpo tagged behind on a loose rein.

Orson said, "Yeah, I stopped by to see you yesterday, but you were gone. By the way, did you know Sage is back? I ran into her at the general store on Saturday. She said she and her aunt, Mrs. Red Elk, returned from Rapid City last Thursday. They're getting ready to repaint the schoolhouse. She said she stopped by to see you a few days ago, but you weren't home. Your grandmother told her that you would be home today. I wouldn't be surprised if she's waiting for you when we get to your grandparents' place."

I thought, *One never knows how the wind will blow. First news about my father, then progress with the roan, and now my friends return home, just when I need them the most.* I could hardly wait to see Sage again.

Friends and Foe

e rounded the last bend toward the cabin, and there she was! Waiting for me, sitting on a stump in the shade of the large cottonwood tree in our front yard. I couldn't believe it. I waved, and she waved back. I could tell from the way she looked at Orson that she was disappointed he was with me. It tickled me to know for once Orson was a thorn in some girl's foot. Orson had a way with the girls and always bragged about how tired he was of girls chasing after him. I doubted that was true. Nevertheless, Sage was different from other girls. She didn't chase after him. Orson knew she could see right through his cat-and-mouse games and that she wanted no part of them.

Her long dark hair was parted on the side. She was wearing it loose around her face. The sunlight caught each strand in shimmering shades of brown that lit up like a halo. She looked just like an angel. She sure looked grown-up, different from our school days, when she wore her hair in braids.

Sage hugged me, and I was surprised how hard I hugged back. Sage and Orson walked with me toward the corrals, telling me about all the things they did on their summer vacations. I unsaddled Anpo and waited for him to cool down before I turned him out to the bigger pasture. I couldn't stop staring at Sage's blue eyes that twinkled in the sunlight. Her pink, bow-perfect mouth crinkled up at the corners when she smiled.

"Alfred! Did you hear me?" my grandmother said. "Please go check on Elmer. He's been at the river with the Bull Elk twins all day. I fear he might be in trouble."

I gave my grandmother a big hug and said, "I'm sorry, Grandmother, I didn't hear you. Yes, I'll check on Elmer as soon as I am finished here."

Orson chimed in. "Hey! If we go check on Elmer, we could go for a swim!"

I said, "Sure. Let's get to the river!"

We raced toward the Missouri River. Usually, Orson's long legs would leave me eating his dust, but I kept neck and neck with him all the way. We reached the riverbank and flopped down on the damp grass, near heat exhaustion. A few minutes later, Sage caught up with us. Panting, she flopped down next to us. We lay there watching the clouds rolling across the sky, looking for shapes of people, animals, and birds.

Turning my head to the right, I shot straight upright. There was Elmer, high up on the limb of a tall dead box elder tree. The Bull Elk twins stood at the bottom of the tree and egged him on.

Elmer shouted when he saw me. "Alfred, look at us. Jerry and Jamie bet me I couldn't reach the top, and I'm almost there!"

I was furious. "Elmer, get down from there immediately. That dead tree could topple over any minute. You need to come down now! You hear? Now!"

Without answering, he scooted down the knotty rotten limbs until his feet were firmly planted on the ground.

Elmer hung his head. "I'm sorry, Alfred. I didn't mean to scare you. I was just showing my friends how brave I was, and you caught me. I'm sorry."

"Go home, Elmer. Grandmother needs your help," I said.

Without hesitation, Elmer skipped down the road toward home with his two mischievous friends on his heels.

We kicked off our shoes and dived off the bank into the cool fresh water below. We swam and caught driftwood as it floated by in the fast current. Only the best swimmers could handle the Missouri

River. My younger brother, Elmer, was not a great swimmer and would have been in trouble if he'd fallen in.

The three of us were tired, and we still had to make the long walk home. The sun turned a hazy yellow, and the wind picked up as clouds of dust rose up. Another dust storm. It swirled through the air and filled the damp crevices of our bodies and clothing. I couldn't believe we'd been squeaky clean just a few minutes ago, and now we looked like mud rats. At this point, we were getting used to the unpredictable weather.

As we walked along, Orson was in a teasing mood.

"Alfred," he said, "remember that time two years ago when Lilly Blue Bird's brother, Alex, stole my new ice skates? He was big, tough, and mean. It looked hopeless, and I thought I'd never get them back. You told me you'd get them back for me. You painted yourself with black and white paint and waited until dark near his outhouse. You looked just like the boggy-creek ghost that supposedly haunts Medicine Creek. When Alex made his evening visit down the path to the outhouse, you stepped out of the darkness. He screamed like a little girl. He thought the boggy-creek ghost had him. He begged for mercy. In a spooky voice, you told him you came for the ice skates, it was wrong to steal, and if he didn't return them, you'd forever haunt him in his dreams. He ran toward his house, stumbling and falling. I was sure he wet his pants. My ice skates mysteriously appeared on my porch the next morning."

We laughed so hard at the image of an almost-grown man running from a make-believe ghost that I almost stumbled on a rock in the middle of the road. We picked up speed to get ahead of the upcoming storm.

Orson said, "My friend, finish telling us about the roan stallion you have been following. I'm sure Sage would love to hear too."

That was all it took to get Sage's attention. Her face lit up like a full moon in October. Sage loved horses. It was her passion to become an equine veterinarian someday. I shared my encounter with the roan stallion and, of course, specific details about my ride inside a fierce tornado.

Orson said, "Wow, my friend. I'm speechless."

"Me too," Sage agreed. "Yes, me too. I am thankful you are still alive. Not very many people survive a tornado, let alone a stallion attack."

I felt safe enough to share the news about my father being alive in the Battle Mountain Sanitarium. They both knew what a sensitive subject it was for me. They listened without a word and waited for a cue from me.

I looked over at Sage, and she said, "We need to pray that he'll recover and make it home to you and his family. It will happen, Alfred. You just have to believe."

I thought how opposite Sage was from me. She was optimistic and sensible. Her faith was as wide as the heavens and could move mountains on earth, I was sure of it. I agreed with Sage and changed the subject.

"I've been riding the roan," I said. "I usually give him a treat, an apple or carrot. It is helping me build trust with him. He's still pretty skittish if he's approached too fast."

I thought this was as good a time as any, so I said, "This summer I have been working at the Looking Rock Ranch for Mr. Karl Looking Rock. He has given me a month off to train the roan. But I plan to go to the ranch tomorrow and check in with him. Would you want to come along and meet the roan, and maybe meet my boss?"

Smiling big and bright, Sage said, "Yippee! Yes, I would! I'm sure my aunt wouldn't mind."

Orson surprised me. "Yes-sir-retee, I would! What time should we meet, old buddy?"

I said, "Let's meet at the Y intersection near Orson's house a bit before high noon."

We shook hands and agreed, and it was official. I watched them walk out of sight and thought how fortunate I was to have such good friends. I was glad my friends were here as I trained for the relay race. I was sure it wouldn't take long to build a training field and get the horses trained, including the blue roan stallion.

Maybe they could also help me find out what Johnny Krugerbery was hiding up his sleeve. No question, my summer had just taken on a whole new meaning.

Three Heads on a Dime

A thick blanket of fog hung over the Missouri River. Rays from the early morning sun skipped across the top of the fog like elk tracks on new-fallen snow. Sage rode her horse, Twila; Orson rode his horse, Blake; and I rode Anpo. We were on our way to Beaver Creek to see the roan, if our luck held out, and then on to the ranch to visit with Karl Looking Rock.

Orson was bored as we rode along, so he decided to pick my brain. "Tell us more about the roan stallion, alias Medicine Hat horse," he said. "I've never seen such a horse, but I've heard many stories. My grandmother told of seeing a Medicine Hat Appaloosa when she was younger. The horse roamed the Badlands between Pine Ridge and Rosebud Agencies. My grandmother said that a Medicine Hat horse is born on a crosshair between the physical world and the spirit world. She said only the bravest warriors could own and ride such a horse."

I told them how I planned to tame the Medicine Hat blue roan stallion and how I needed their help. I told them about the horse relay races at the White River Frontier Days and how I planned to win the relay and buy my grandfather a new tractor.

I was surprised they both said to count them in. We stayed on the subject of the roan all the way to Beaver Creek. We waited patiently for signs of the roan from my usual spot. I was starting to think the roan might not show up today, but then the fog dissipated as the heat from the sun increased. Sage was the first one to spot the band.

"There he is, the blue roan stallion. The legendary Medicine Hat horse," she whispered. "Wow! He's a beauty. Look at the way he is holding his head. What a fine horse."

This was a high review of the roan coming from Sage. Sage had attended horse-training school in Kansas City, Missouri. She knew a lot about horse behaviors. We were lucky to have her on our team. Unlike me, she was focused and responsible: two traits that were needed to be a good horse trainer. I was glad Sage was eager to help train the roan stallion. Besides, I really liked her company. Her presence would keep me from my daydreams and focused on the tasks at hand.

The roan circled his band of mares, strutting, snorting, and throwing his massive head from side to side. I moved away from Orson and Sage to mask their scents.

I saw him stop grazing and whistled through my teeth. "Tweeeeeeet!"

He lifted his head and moved his ears forward. I whistled again, and he started toward me. He knew I had treats, and most of all, he knew I would not hurt him. I coaxed him toward me; he snorted and danced and came closer. He was so close I could smell his breath. I slowly reached up and touched his mane. He snorted. I assumed he smelled Sage and Orson on me. I gently touched his mane until he calmed down and let my hand rest there a bit longer.

Satisfied everything was okay, the roan settled down. I slipped his rope halter and reins on over his head. In a split second, I slid up on his sleek bare back. I always rode the roan bareback, without a saddle. I tugged on the reins.

The roan twitched, then shot across the open field like a cannonball at the state fair. We made a couple of passes in front of Sage and Orson. All I could see was the blur of their gaping faces. Feeling the roan slow down, I figured it was time to end our ride. I slid off the roan and walked him around until he cooled down.

I motioned Sage and Orson toward us. The roan didn't like the unfamiliar scents a single bit. He yanked back on the reins. I held him tight until he settled down. Sage knew just what to do. She cooed and talked to him in her lullaby voice.

"Hey, Beautiful One. You sure are one fine stallion. I am so happy to meet you."

The roan loved it. He stood perfectly still. The way the roan responded to Sage's soft voice made me wonder if his previous owner was female.

I removed his reins and gave him his usual treats, apples. He gobbled the apples up before I could say jack-splat. He snorted in contentment and galloped toward his band without looking back. Sage and Orson were flabbergasted.

Sage said, "Alfred, that was incredible. How long have you been riding him?"

Giving her a wide grin, I said, "I've been working with the roan for most of the summer. I want to start building our training field and start training the horses. We don't have much time left."

We mounted our horses and headed toward the Looking Rock Ranch. Hopefully, we would reach the ranch by noon. Riding by the creek below the ranch, I had a strange sensation that we were being watched. I stopped and scanned the dark shadows along the tree line, but I couldn't see anything odd. But the feeling wouldn't leave me.

Orson said, "Alfred, what are the dates for the White River Frontier Days?"

"Friday, August first; Saturday, August second; and Sunday, August third. I heard this might be the last time for the celebration and gala," I answered.

Sage was surprised. "What! Why?"

I replied, "Karl Looking Rock told me that the town of White River has decided to make this their last year. That's probably why the winning pot is extra big this year."

Sage said, "That's too bad. I attended the White River Frontier Days twice with my mother and my aunt. It only cost us a dime for the entire family to have fun. They had a Wild West show, a carnival, lots of food and dancing, airplane rides, and a most impressive horse relay run. I remember the race like it was yesterday. It was exhilarating. I was practically jumping off the grandstand. My aunt said that Indian relay racing is part of our spiritual horse traditions that are well over five hundred years old."

Orson lifted his floppy straw hat and scratched his head. "How were the teams set up?"

Sage said, "Each rider starts in front of the grandstands and mounts his horse bareback from a standing position. I think each team has four people: a rider, two holders, and a mugger. The rider makes three laps around the racetrack and switches to a different horse at the end of each lap."

Sage continued, "The holders hold the horses and keep them calm between exchanges. The mugger catches the incoming horse and helps the rider jump to the next horse and continue the race. The timers keep track of the time. The teams with the best times advance to the final race the next day. The winning relay team wins the relay and the cash pot."

Orson looked confused. "That confirms it. We're one team member short. Maybe we can get Junior White Hail to help us. He's not doing anything, just hanging out with his grandmother."

I said, "I think that's a great plan, Orson. Since it was your idea, Sage and I just nominated you to go find Junior and convince him to join our team."

Chuckling, Orson agreed.

Horse Thief

By the time we reached the Looking Rock Ranch, it was high noon. Our ride together had given us the opportunity to visit and make plans. Now came the hard work, building the training track and training the horses. We rode straight to the stables to take care of our horses. We removed our sweat-soaked saddles and gear to let them dry out from the long ride.

I said, "Follow me to the tack house. We will put our saddles inside to dry."

Orson said, "I've always thrown my saddle over the fence railing and let it dry out in the sun."

I said, "Heck, buddy, that could be the reason your saddle is dried up and brittle. My father told me it will ruin wet saddles, gloves, and leather chaps if you let them dry in the direct sunlight. Besides, Karl Looking Rock makes the most incredible neat's-foot oil. My saddle soaked the oil up nicely, and now it's super soft."

Orson didn't like to be corrected. "You convinced me, Schoolteacher Alfred Which-cha-ma-call-it."

I said, "Come on, Orson, you don't need to be a mad boar about it. Just passing on some elder wisdom . . ."

My voice trailed off as a shadow in the sunlight-filled doorway of the tack house distracted me. I spun around, thinking that spooky old Johnny Krugerbery was sneaking up on me again. It was only Cheyenne, one of Karl Looking Rock's ranch hands.

"Karl wants to see you kids when you're finished here. He's over there." Cheyenne pointed his stained gloved finger toward the main house.

"Thanks. No problem," I said.

I knew Karl Looking Rock would be thrilled to finally meet my friends. As much as I talked about them, he practically knew them already.

Karl was waiting for us. He sat on his front porch swing, holding a glass of mint tea. "Son, you and your friends come over here and sit with me."

The worried look in his eyes told me that Karl Looking Rock was very bothered by something.

"Martha," Karl said to a gray-haired woman who wore a starched white apron and a big friendly smile. "This is Alfred, the young man I told you about, and his friends . . . ?"

I said, "Shucks, I'm sorry. These are my friends Sage and Orson."

Karl knew their names already, given the countless stories I'd told him. I was sure he was reminding us about proper elder etiquette.

Karl said, "I'm pleased to meet you two young'uns. This is Alfred's home away from home. And I want you two to feel the same way. Please, make yourselves comfortable."

Sage replied, "Thank you, Mr. Looking Rock. We are very honored to meet you as well. And thank you for welcoming us to your beautiful home."

With a bright voice, Martha said, "I'm Martha, Karl's cousin. My husband, Pete, is in the kitchen. We have been taking care of the cooking for the ranch for the past thirty years. My cousin Karl has told me so much about you, Alfred, and your friends too."

Martha turned around at the door. "Oh goodness, I forgot to ask you if you would like a glass of water or tea before lunch."

"I would love a glass of tea. Thank you. And I'm happy to meet you too," we all said at the same time, laughing at our timing.

Martha gave us a wink and disappeared through the wooden screen door.

Karl Looking Rock looked to make sure we were alone. Leaning forward, he said, "Alfred, it's okay if your friends hear this. I wanted to warn you about my nephew Johnny. I believe he's up to no good."

Karl's face paled. He stood up and paced back and forth along the length of the front porch. "Alfred, do you remember me telling you about the stock market crashing last October?"

I said, "I sure do."

Karl continued, "They called it Black Monday. That incident created an agriculture depression that impacted me and the rest of the farmers and ranchers in the Midwest. Many banks were foreclosing, and people were losing their homes and investments in droves. I managed to hold on to my investments and ranch with the help of my dear friend Mr. Arthur Freelove. Arthur is a banker at the First National Bank in Kennebec, and we have been friends for many years. He guided me through the crash."

Karl stopped to sip his tea, then continued, "Last week, Sheriff Hoffer delivered a message from Arthur. He wanted to meet with me. Expecting the worst news, I dreaded the visit. What I heard was not what I expected to hear. Arthur said that my nephew Johnny presented him with a forged withdrawal slip. He was trying to withdraw ten thousand dollars from my cash safety deposit box. When Arthur asked him why, Johnny said I was deeply concerned about the First National Bank's financial ability to withstand a failing economic market. Arthur refused the note and told Johnny to tell me to come in to see him in person. I never knew about Arthur's invitation until Sheriff Hoffer showed up. It gets worse. Yesterday I went into the bank and met with Arthur . . ."

Martha interrupted Karl's story when she returned with our tea and shortbread cookies. After seeing Karl's tense posture, she figured he needed to be alone with us. She said, "You kids enjoy the tea. I wish I could sit and visit, but I have a lot to do to get lunch ready. So I will see you all later."

Jumping up, Sage followed Martha to the kitchen. "I would love to help you, Martha. I'm a very good cook."

Martha replied, "Excellent, it would be wonderful to have a pretty young girl help me instead of my old husband, Cranky Pete."

Upon hearing his name, Pete stuck his thin face out of the open window. "What cha want, Marty?"

Martha shooed him back with her dish towel. "Never mind, Pete. I was just saying how nice it was to have extra help in my kitchen today."

Their voices faded into silence, like the silence before a storm.

Karl's voiced dropped to a whisper. "Arthur showed me a wanted poster with a picture of my nephew Johnny on the front. Johnny Krugerbery is wanted for stealing cattle and horses, wrongful branding, and crossing and reselling the stolen cattle and horses in surrounding states. When Johnny found out that I knew about his scheme, he left the ranch with several of my guns and extra ammunition. Three of the ranch hands that came with him when he moved here also left."

Karl stood up and started pacing the length of the porch again. "I believe Johnny is holed up nearby and brewing up trouble. Alfred, I know Johnny didn't like you from the start. I figured you sensed something that I didn't. I think in some odd way, Johnny has blamed you for his foiled scheme to take over my ranch. I don't want you to get hurt. Martha, Pete, and I will be moving into town for the next three weeks until we get this resolved. Cheyenne, Bird Man, and Jacob have agreed to stay here and take care of my horses. I will be coming back during the day to check on things. It's best you stay away from here until I get back. I'm planning to make it to the White River Frontier Days in a few weeks to serve as your relay team sponsor."

It wasn't the news I'd expected to hear today. Nevertheless, I respected Karl Looking Rock's honesty and the trust he had in me.

Putting that daunting news aside, we had a blast. Karl showed us some of his special antique collections. Martha shared her recipes with Sage and gifted her a beautiful embroidered apron from Germany. The day passed much too soon, and it was time to start home. I felt an awful dread leaving the ranch. Like something bad was going to happen, something I couldn't stop.

We rode back to Iron Nation under a cloud of worry for Karl Looking Rock.

I said, "I guess now would be a good time for us to get started on building a training camp for our horses."

Orson reminded us that we needed to make sure Junior was on board with us. He said, "I will stop by Grandmother White Hail's cabin this evening and ask Junior if he wants to join our team."

We all agreed that getting Junior on our team was the first step. We agreed to meet late tomorrow morning at our usual spot, the intersection at the Y in the road.

The setting sun rolled out a beautiful vermillion blanket across the western sky. Dust swirled under me in circles. Out of nowhere, I missed Chepa.

"Giddyup, Anpo Boy. Let's get home," I said as I urged Anpo into a trot.

Just Build It!
Okay

I drove my grandfather's team, pulled by Sally and Sadie, toward the Y intersection in the road to meet my friends. Chepa followed behind, and Elmer sat perched next to me in the high wagon seat. Elmer was excited and talked nonstop. I'd promised my mother I would keep a close eye on Elmer while she was away. He would just have to tag along with me. Maybe I could find something for him to do, anything to keep him out of trouble.

I thought, *Jumping fish lips! I think I found the perfect fit for Elmer.*

I said to him, "Hey, little brother, would you like to be the referee for our relay team?"

"Sure, but what is a referee, and what will I be doing?" Elmer answered.

"You will be the person that makes sure the relay team members follow the rules. This is a very important team position. During a real relay race, breaking a rule will disqualify a team from the race," I answered.

Perking up, Elmer said, "What rules are you talking about?"

I scooted closer so he could hear me better. "The first rule is making sure all the relay team members start their positions with both feet on the ground. The second rule is keeping other team members from touching the rider when he or she is mounting or dismounting. I'll share more important rules later."

"Jumping mice beans! This job sounds hard and not so fun. I think you need to pay me, Alfred." Elmer's serious face almost made me start laughing out loud.

"Of course, I will pay you if we win. For now, let's build the practice field and make it happen."

We pulled up next to Sage, Orson, and Junior White Hail waiting for us on horseback.

I smiled broadly at my friends. "Thanks, everyone, for coming. Thank you, Junior, for joining our team. I hope your grandmother is doing good."

Grandmother White Hail was a traditional elder very much respected in our community. She'd raised Junior since he was a baby after the accidental death of his parents.

Junior said, "Thank you, Alfred. My grandmother is doing good for being seventy-five years old. She has been staying active, sewing star quilts, collecting medicinal plants, and caring for her chickens."

"Great to hear that, Junior. Okay, team! Let's get with it. We have a long day ahead," I said.

Junior's dog, Jaber Boy, ran ahead of us with Chepa, and they playfully nipped at each other.

I tugged lightly on the reins. It didn't take very much effort to get Sally and Sadie moving up the hill.

"Get up there, girls! Haw, turn left . . . now steady ahead."

We established one corner of the pasture as our headquarters. It was shaded and close to the spring. After we unloaded the wagon, we made our prayers with tobacco offerings. I looked across the pasture and marveled at prairie grass swaying in the hot summer breeze. Golden waves as far as my eyes could see. The starkness of the barbwire fences cutting through nature's serenity stirred my emotions.

My spirit stone moved against my chest. Above us, a golden eagle glided flawlessly through the air currents. It was my spirit helper; the golden eagle helped carry our prayers to the Creator. The moment made me remember the day I helped my grandfather build this pasture fence. He told me never to forget the old ways. Deep in thought, I could hear Grandfather's words:

"In the old days there were no fences and no land ownership, and the buffalo were plenty. Now we find ourselves fenced in like prisoners on reservations. The government issues us a card telling us that we are Indians, as if we don't know who we are. We are the People, the allies. They ask us to show them this card in order to get food to feed our starving babies. They ask us to show them this card if we want permission to leave our fenced-in reservation. They want to know where we are going and when we will return. Maybe they approve the request, maybe not. If we are late returning, we become an escaped savage on the run. Inside the fenced-in reservations, they gave us small parcels. Giving us our own land back? The land where my people hunted our buffalo and cared for our babies? I don't understand. They expect us to be farmers, to grow crops from the poor seeds they give us, but the crops often die. They expect us to be ranchers and fight over land they gave us. But the sick cattle they send to replace the buffalo they killed often die. They expect us to build fences on the land they gave us, so here we are, Grandson . . . building fences."

Sage waved her hand in front of my face. "Oh, Alfreeeed . . . wake up."

Startled from my daydream, I said, "I'm sorry. Let's get busy and build a training track!"

I steered the plow behind Sally and tipped the blade evenly over the ground. With each pass, many rocks were uncovered. Junior and Elmer stacked the rocks along the fence line. The pasture was cleared and leveled in no time. Orson diverted a small amount of water from a nearby spring and packed the loose soil down to make a smooth surface.

We decided to let the damp ground set overnight. Tomorrow we would start racing Anpo, Blake, Twila, and Junior's horse, Buffalo Thunder, together as a team. We planned to introduce the roan into the team next week.

The relay team members wanted to know their roles, so we sat in a circle under the shade of a cottonwood tree and made our plans. We decided that I would be the rider to make the three required laps around the track. In each lap, I would ride a different horse. Orson would be our mugger. He would wave me down and catch my horse as I rode in. Junior would be our holder man, keeping the second horse ready for the second lap. Sage would be our back-up holder. Last but not least, Elmer would be our referee, helping us all follow the relay rules and avoid being disqualified.

We moved on to discussing the sequence of our horses and decided Anpo would race the first lap. His calm nature would set the pace for the required exchanges between horses. We decided Blake would race the second lap, and the roan stallion would race the third lap. The roan's speed and stamina would push us toward the big win. If we needed to rotate our horses, Twila and Buffalo Thunder would be available.

Throwing my right arm up with a closed fist, I shouted, "Hey, team! We can do this!"

A number of raised arms followed in unison. "Heck yes! Let's do it!"

The week passed quickly, and the horses worked great together. They learned how to stand still until we said, "Whoa." We walked them in circles to purposely limit the movement of their legs. They were also getting used to the obstacles, such as oak barrels we placed at the sides of the track that simulated distractions.

Every day, after finishing chores at home, the relay team members met at the pasture. Training started with exercises that helped the horses develop endurance for more speed.

We created a false storm of tension, where I would mount and dismount from one horse to the next one. This was done until the horses became used to it and stayed calm during the transitions. This would help in the real race when I needed to change horses on the run.

Elmer memorized all the relay rules, and he made sure we followed them to a tee. It was summertime, and I was sure he missed hanging out with his friends, the Bull Elk twins. But he stayed strong in his duty.

After we broke for lunch, the team would stay and continue training the horses while I rode to Beaver Creek to train the roan for two hours. I would rejoin the team at our headquarters before we broke for the day. The roan was making better progress than I expected. It was obvious he had been trained by someone at one time. It didn't take him long to remember basic commands.

The breakthrough for the roan finally came. He kept calm during my maneuvers, and when I leaped on his back, jumped off, and leaped back on again and again, it didn't bother him. He stood still and relaxed. It was time to introduce the roan to the rest of the team and start a new journey.

Practice Makes Perfect

Do you think the coaching and exercises will really help the horses learn how to relay race?" asked Elmer.

"Certainly," I said. "By running every day, they should develop endurance and faster run speeds. Our mounting and dismounting from Anpo to Blake to Twila to Buffalo Thunder and back around again helps the horses get desensitized and stay calm during the transitions, which can get pretty chaotic. This will be necessary in the real relay race, when I'll be changing horses on the run."

The hot midday sun created a glare that lay over the pasture, making everything look golden and hazy.

"Woo-hoo! Food and water break time!" hollered Elmer.

Sage spread out a blanket under the shade of the lone twisted willow tree. She unloaded the basket of goodies that Grandmother had sent with us. The horses relaxed in the shade near the spring and munched away on dried brown prairie grass.

"I'm going to ride on to Beaver Creek and work with the roan stallion. Do you all mind staying here and continuing our coaching regimen with the horses? I'll be back in a couple of hours," I said.

"Sure!"

"No problem."

"Can I go with you?"

"No. Elmer, you can't go with me. I'll be back soon."

No sooner did I show up in my usual spot than the roan made his way up the embankment to meet me. I was thrilled; we were making better progress than I expected. It wasn't taking him long to learn basic commands. I was certain the roan had gotten some training sometime in his mysterious past. *Where did he come from? How did he end up here?* I suspected his progress all hinged on trust.

The roan kept calm during my relay transition maneuvers. Starting on foot, I leaped on his back, jumped off, and leaped back on again and again. It didn't bother him as much as it had yesterday. He stood still and relaxed. I thought, *Whew, about time. I think we're ready for the next step. I will start him with the other horses tomorrow.*

Putting my full body against him so he could feel the rise and fall of my breathing, I said, "Blue

Boy, tomorrow it's time to start your new adventure and introduce you to the rest of our team."

The roan nickered, and I had a feeling he understood me.

That night, as I lay in my bed, I could hear the hum of a thousand mosquitoes clinging to the screened-in walls encircling the front porch. I thought about how hard it was going to be to leave Chepa at home when the time came to bring the roan to Iron Nation pasture. I was sure we'd figure it out.

Daybreak came much too soon. Chester, Grandmother's highest-ranking rooster, performed his daily duty to break the dawn and let the world know he was king of the roost. "Cock-a-doodle-do . . . Cock-a-doodle-do . . ."

I rose out of bed and stumbled bleary-eyed toward the outhouse. I filled the tin basin on the back-porch table with cold water and doused my face. *GASP!* I was wide awake. I followed the smell of fresh coffee and the sound of sizzling bacon toward the kitchen. Grandfather, Grandmother, and Elmer were seated around the round oak table. Blue cedar and sage smoke hung in the log rafters, remnants of routine morning prayers.

"Good morning, Grandson," Grandfather said. "Hope you had a good night."

I nodded I did.

"Wanted to let you know that your mother sent us a telegram yesterday. She said to tell you and Elmer that your father's health is slowly improving day by day. She still doesn't know if or when he will get to come home."

I nodded again. I was having a hard time believing my father was really alive. Perhaps it would be different if I saw him in person. I sure wasn't going to get my hopes up too much, lest I be let down again. If he was really alive, he'd come home. Otherwise, it was a made-up story to me . . . just a made-up story meant to give me false hope.

Grandmother said, "Are you taking Elmer with you today?"

"He sure is. I've been a big help to our team," Elmer piped up. "Huh, Alfred?"

"Yes, little brother, I wouldn't know what to do without you," I said, winking at Grandmother.

Grandmother smiled back at me and continued clearing the table. "Don't forget the basket of food I packed for you and your friends." She motioned toward the table near the door.

"I won't. Thank you," I said. "Come on, Elmer, let's finish our chores and get going. Today is a big day."

I thought to myself, *Yippee, the roan is finally going to join our team and start training with the other horses.*

Orson, Sage, and Junior were leaning against a pile of weathered cedar fence posts, waiting at the pasture. They knew today would be a challenge for me. Sage volunteered to bring me to the roan on her horse. We rode toward Beaver Creek, with me riding behind her on her horse. As we rode, I felt her body move against me with each of the horse's movements. Her hair smelled of the wild basil we called Indian perfume. I had a hard time keeping my mind on the roan. I knew Sage felt it too. I decided at that moment that someday, when we were older, I was going to marry her . . .

"Alfred, did you hear me? Is that the roan waiting by the fence?" Sage said.

Her voice jarred me out of my daydream. "Yes, it sure is. He is becoming a creature of habit."

I slid off Twila and walked up to the roan. He greeted me with a whinny and nudged my arm.

"Whoa there, Blue Boy, slow down."

I gave him his favorite treat, an apple and two carrots. In no time, he was haltered up and ready to be ridden bareback. I jumped onto his back, and we followed Sage and Twila back toward the training pasture.

The pasture gate swung open, and the roan stallion lunged through, laying his ears back. He resisted the lead rope in my hand, but I held on tight. The roan's energy was intense. A whirlwind picked up some dust and swirled it around us. I could feel his uncertainty. His muzzle quivered, and he rolled his blue eyes until the whites were showing.

His flank twitched nervously. He did not like being in the company of the other horses and the rest of our team. I walked the roan in circles, talking him down and using a gentle touch. To make matters worse, the other horses smelled the roan's strong musk scent and responded by trying to create distance between them and the roan. The chaos played out for the next hour. I continued to work with the roan as Orson, Sage, and Junior inched their horses closer to him. We were determined to make all the horses feel more at ease.

Back in my memory, I saw a boy from a long time ago who lived with his family along the Missouri River in the old way. His father gave him a young mustang gelding. The mustang was a beautiful paint but one of the wildest horses the boy had ever seen. The boy's father instructed him not to get near the mustang alone.

The boy was determined to tame the mustang and make him his own. One day when his father was away from home, the boy decided to ride the mustang. He tied a rope around the mustang's neck, and grabbing a handful of horse mane, he threw his body over the back of the mustang. The shock surged through him like a lightning bolt. The mustang's first lunge jolted the boy to his gut and sucked away his breath.

Each thrust pounded through the boy's spine until he thought he was going to break into a million pieces. He hung on to the mustang's mane with all his might. One final desperate lunge, but the boy stayed on the mustang's back. The mustang began to relax, but the boy was too frightened to stop and get off, so he rode the mustang around and around until his father returned a short time later. His father was surprised to see his son riding the wild mustang.

The boy's father said, "Son, I'm disappointed you disobeyed me. The Great Spirit has given you a gift to communicate with the horse nation. But you must learn discernment of heart and discipline of your mind. They will make a way for you through your life."

That young boy was me, and I knew it was time to use my gift.

All Is Lost

As I laid my head against the roan's shoulder and felt the heat of the sun against my back, I focused on a place deep inside of the roan, his spirit. I told him he had nothing to fear, that I would never put him in harm's way. I told him I needed his help and cooperation. I told him about my dream to win the upcoming relay race for my grandfather, and I told him that he was the key to my dream and winning the race.

Training the horses now took on a different atmosphere. The horses were getting used to one another. By the end of the week, we had the horses standing still and calm during mounting and dismounting. Time passed much too quickly. I couldn't believe that we were four days out from the big race. I wondered if we were ready, but I supposed we were as ready as we could be. It was time to get ourselves and our horses to White River Fairgrounds.

Pink clouds skirted across the sky. Grandfather, Grandmother, Elmer, and Sage headed south to the White River before the morning sun peeked over the eastern ridge. They'd planned to get a jump start on the crowds and set up camp in a good spot near the river. They were riding with Uncle Jay in his Chevy one-ton grain truck. The bed of the truck was packed with a canvas tepee and poles, two box tents, a small cooking stove, and plenty of groceries.

Orson, Junior, and I rode our horses over to Looking Rock Ranch. Karl Looking Rock was taking us and our horses to White River. He had a brand-new brown REO FD Master Speed Wagon truck. The truck had a 268-cubic-inch, 67-horsepower six-cylinder engine. Hitched to it was a trailer for the horses. Karl said it was the fastest truck of its kind and it would get us to White River in one day.

Karl was our team sponsor. He said we needed to be at the fairgrounds to register the day before the race to ensure our slot. It was going to be a seventy-mile trip, so the REO FD Master Speed Wagon would do just fine to get us there on time.

We decided to leave Sage's horse, Twila, and use only Buffalo Thunder in case Anpo or Blake needed a break. I was in the lead on Anpo, leading the roan with a rope in one hand and Anpo's reins in the other. Orson followed me on his horse, Blake, and Junior was coming up in the rear on his horse, Buffalo Thunder.

As soon as we cleared the hill and started down toward the ranch, I could tell something was wrong. Karl's horses were crammed into the small holding stalls. That happened only on branding day or under unusual circumstances.

From a grove of trees, we watched two trucks pull out of the ranch onto the main road. They were loaded with numerous oak barrels. Whoever was driving had left the main gate open behind them. Karl and his hired ranch hands would never do that. We looked for signs of Karl Looking Rock, but he was nowhere to be seen. I feared the worst.

"We must get a better look. Let's go to the hayloft in the barn. We'll have a good view of the ranch from that location," I said.

We led Anpo, Blake, Buffalo Thunder, and the roan behind the lower bunkhouse near the creek and tied them in the bushes so they were hidden. We made our way to the barn and slipped quietly up the ladder into the loft.

Two strange men loaded more barrels into another truck. I'd always had a gut feeling that Johnny Krugerbery had plans to run a horse-rustling setup at the Looking Rock Ranch. It appeared he was also running a bootlegging operation. My question was, *Where is Karl Looking Rock? Is he okay?*

"Well now! What a surprise . . . three little Injuns, all lined up and looking like three spooked tweedle birds."

My heart jumped right up my throat. Johnny Krugerbery's stocky shadow loomed over us. He was holding a Thompson submachine gun snuggly under his right arm. His snaggled-toothed grin sent a chill right down my spine. I knew we were in danger. Johnny was deadly. I feared he would do everything in his power to hurt me and my friends.

In the most convincing voice I could muster up, I said, "Hello, Johnny. Just showing my friends around. Mr. Looking Rock wanted me to show up today and help him clean saddles . . . and . . ."

A strike to my gut from the butt of the tommy gun dropped me to my knees.

"I know you're lying, boy. Uncle Karl skipped town. He went bonkers after he lost all his money in the foreclosure at the First National Bank. Had to tie him up to keep him from hurting himself. So sad for the old man. But that's the way the ball bounces. Get yourselves down from here, now!" Johnny knocked Orson facedown in the hay and kept his boot on Orson's head. "Don't get any ideas, pretty boy. I'll shoot you full of holes before you know what hit you. Now get up, and make it quick. I don't have all day. Get going, all of you. Now!"

Orson scrambled down the ladder. Junior and I followed close behind.

Johnny marched us around the corner of the barn with his tommy gun aimed at our backs. He pushed us along the path toward the main house. I stumbled and fell on something. In the bloody grass under me was a man facedown. Johnny kicked the man and turned him over on his back. It was Curly Jake, Johnny Krugerbery's sidekick. His eyes were fixed straight ahead. He had a bullet hole in his chest. His clothes were muddy and torn, like he'd been in a bad fight. He was definitely dead. My heart was in my throat.

Johnny said, "I reckon you get the idea. I mean business. No fancy stuff, and we'll get along just fine. YOU HEAR?"

I looked down at the bloody grass under Curly Jake and nodded. I understood clearly. I was struck by a frightful thought. *Did he kill Karl Looking Rock the same way he killed Curly Jake? Is Johnny going to kill us? No. I must keep a clear head. We are very much alive now, and I aim to keep us alive!*

When we reached the main house, Johnny kicked the screen door open and pushed us inside, knocking us to the floor.

I could hear muffled voices in the dim light. I recognized Karl Looking Rock's voice. My eyes adjusted to the light. Martha and Pete were tied at the ankles and wrists, sitting up against the dining room wall next to Karl. Both had rags stuffed in their mouths.

"Come on now, nephew. Whatever you want, just let me know. But please don't hurt these kids. They haven't done a darn thing to you," Karl said.

Johnny said, "Shut up, old man! You talk too much! I told you twice to just shut up before I bash your head in!"

We heard a dull thud, and Karl toppled back against the wall, dazed. I scrambled to my feet to try and help him.

Ugh! I felt the wind leave my solar plexus as Johnny Krugerbery's boot kicked me so hard he lifted me off the floor and slammed me back down.

"Alfred Swallow, you are one dumb Injun kid. You don't listen to reason, do you? Sure, not my fault." Johnny Krugerbery snickered above me.

Another boot kick, and everything went black.

The Big Day

When I opened my burning eyes, I found Junior tied up and pushed up next to Karl, Martha, and Pete to my left. I looked for Orson. He was sprawled out in a limp heap next to me. I spied a rifle leaned up against a table where a thin man with a black beard sat. I assumed it was one of Johnny's gang members. I thought, *If only I could ease myself across the wooden floor, maybe I could grab the rifle.* I knew it was wishful thinking as soon as I tried to move and couldn't. My wrists were bound tight by a single rope.

A smashing and thumping sound on the porch grew louder. *Whack! Thwogg! Wap!* The hinges on the wooden porch screen door creaked, and two men crashed into the room in a tangled ball of flying fists and boots. It was Cheyenne, Karl's trusted ranch hand, fighting with Johnny Krugerbery. The thin man with the black beard jumped into the mix. I feared Cheyenne was a goner when Johnny wrapped both of his hands tightly around his neck.

I knew I had to act fast and scooted up next to Orson. I whispered, "Reach into my back pocket and get my Swiss Army knife and cut the rope off my wrists. Hurry!"

Orson sawed away at the rope until it finally gave way. He threw the knife toward Junior. "Free yourself and the others."

Without a second to spare, I was on Johnny's back, trying to save Cheyenne's life. Orson tackled the black-bearded man, and all four of us heaved and rolled across the floor. Cheyenne, coughing and sputtering, jumped to his feet just as Johnny's outstretched fingers found his gun.

Too late, Johnny pulled the trigger just as I rolled to the side. A deafening round of bullets sprayed the ceiling. Cheyenne knocked Johnny's gun away and pinned him to the floor. Grabbing a remnant of rope, I helped Cheyenne tie Johnny's wrists together. Orson and Junior already had the black-bearded man's tied up as well.

Cheyenne threw me a rifle. "Keep an eye on them," he said. "I'm going to check on the others."

Cheyenne disappeared out the door. Within seconds, he returned with Bird Man and Jack. They had four of Johnny's gang members tied to the porch banisters. Just in the nick of time. A black Ford Model A Paddy Wagon with a white star on the door and a red light turning on top drove up in the front yard. It was Sheriff Hoffer; his deputy, Dallas; and Jacob, Karl's hired ranch hand.

Cheyenne told Sheriff Hoffer what had happened. "We rode in from town in time to see Johnny marching Alfred and his friends toward the main house with a gun to their backs. We knew all heck had broken loose. We sent Jacob into town to get you all out here. I would say you all made it here just in time."

We all agreed. Johnny and his gang were loaded into the paddy wagon with long faces. Sheriff Hoffer said he would book them and keep them under guard at the jailhouse in Kennebec tonight. Tomorrow he would transport them to Pierre for trial.

Pete kindled the wood cookstove and heated water for us to wash the crusted blood off our faces and hands. Martha heated up a pot of stew from the icebox. She said, "Just want to give you kids all a good meal. It will help you feel better. I don't understand how this all happened, but thank the Lord those crooks are in the hands of Sheriff Hoffer."

We all nodded in agreement, but our eyes were focused on the pot bubbling away on the top of the stove. With Martha's good meal under our belts, we were almost back to normal.

Karl could not thank us enough for helping them. He reminded us, "We need to get going if we want to pull into the camp before sunset."

Bird Man and Jack fetched Anpo, Blake, Buffalo Thunder, and the roan.

Karl said, "That roan has the look of an eagle. He's one fine horse." Of course I agreed wholeheartedly.

Bird Man and Jack helped load our horses into the back of Karl's REO FD Master Speed Wagon truck. The side rails were sturdy and fairly high, and the horses were securely tied to the rails. The roan was the only horse having a problem with riding in the back of the truck. I had to watch him closely.

We stopped in Murdo to water and walk the horses. We were making good time. Karl figured we would be in White River at sundown. I reckoned we'd be as ready as we could be after a good sleep.

I spotted Uncle Jay's truck next to Grand-mother's tepee on the south side of the fairgrounds. Grandfather, Grandmother, Elmer, and Sage were happy to see us but mortified by the story we shared. Elmer had me repeat it several times.

Karl immediately left for the main tent to register our team, Iron Nation Relay Team, and to pay our fee.

Orson, Sage, Junior, and I found a good spot behind our tents to keep the horses. Although there were stables for the horses, we wanted to keep them close by. We sat by the river, visiting and just having a good time. The smell of campfires hung thick in the air. The blended sound of children playing, animal noises, the babbling of the river, and people laughing, namely Sage, relaxed me and filled me with a magical feeling, like something wonderful was about to happen.

The whinny of our horses awakened me. They were hungry and so was I. The big day was finally here.

The grandstands filled early, long before any regular events began. The crowd waited patiently for the races to start. Fairgoers were trickling in. They paid five cents per adult at the gate for admission.

The White River Frontier Days fair officially opened with an address by Mayor Lyle McFadden, followed by a welcome from Marvin Geddes, president of the White River Frontier Days board. Music was provided by the Mellette Quartet, and they kicked off the event with a snappy tune. After the welcoming, the fairgoers spread out like ants looking for sugar.

The events included a Wild West carnival with boxing matches, a rodeo with bulldogging, saddle and bareback bronc riding, bull riding, greased pig races for the children, a harness race, a baseball tournament, airplane rides and parachute leap shows, a women's wagon race, and relay races on horseback for men and women. All winners were paid with hefty purses.

Exhibit tents were set up along the west side. They included the finest swine, sheep, poultry, horses, and mules, as well as booths with baked and canned goods, dried meats and fruit, and recipe cook-offs. Prizes of seventy-five cents were awarded for first place.

Karl came back with our schedule. He said, "Okay, young'uns, the race starts in about two hours. Let's pick up speed and get over to the grandstands early."

Grandfather and Karl helped us wrap the horses' legs from the knee and hock down. The wrapping helped support their tendons and ligaments and kept horseflies off their legs.

Junior, Orson, and Elmer painted all four horses with our team colors, red and blue. Red circles were painted around their eyes, a red handprint on their left shoulders, and blue lightning bolts on both flanks. Anpo, Blake, and the roan were our main horses. In case we needed to replace one of them, we had Buffalo Thunder on standby.

Grandmother helped paint us. We dressed in matching Native regalia: leather leggings tied over our pants, beaded moccasins, and ribbon shirts, except for me. I was bare chested and had the lower half of my legs wrapped like the horses to avoid any hang-ups during mounting and dismounting.

Grandmother adorned us with various beaded medallions, armbands, and headbands. We all wore our hair loose, with eagle feathers braided in for protection. Sage wore a large white eagle plume in her hair.

Grandfather painted lightning bolts on my face and chest with red-earth paint. I thought, *How did he know? These markings are just like the ones in my dream.*

He offered a prayer to the Great Spirit for our safety and smudged us and our horses with cedar, sage, and sweetgrass.

Grandfather said, "Please remember, an Indian relay race is deeper than winning a purse of money. You're reliving an old tradition and a connection to our horse nation relatives. The race involves teamwork, expert horsemanship, pageantry, and possible misfortune at every turn. You need to stay alert at all times. Go out there and do your best to compete, but remember to ride honest, clean, and fair."

"Hoka!" I was ready to ride.

Relay Day

he announcer called for the teams to take their posts at the starting line marked across the track in front of the grandstand. I led Anpo out and stood alongside him, waiting for a signal to start. The crowd loved the pageantry and went wild. Anpo's eyes were as big and round as Grandmother's handheld looking glass. Orson and Sage held Blake and the roan stallion. Junior and Elmer held Buffalo Thunder, just in case. We were one of seven teams parading past the grandstand: Little River, Dancing Road, Rising Voice, Medicine Butte, Crow Hop, Cherry Creek, and us, Iron Nation.

Each rider was dressed in Native regalia and had a whip in one hand and the reins of the lead horse in his other. All the horses were bareback. All the riders waited with bated breath. I focused on my vision of galloping across the heavens among the stars. I believed this was the time.

The crack of a gunshot pierced the air. Each rider leaped from a standing position with both feet on the ground onto his horse's back. I felt the extreme rush of adrenaline as we raced past the tepees and spectators that lined the track. Dust swirled and rose up in our wake. Excitement ramped up. The Rising Voice and Crow Hop teams had the lead. The horses were bunched together heading up the back stretch. I rubbed my hand up and down Anpo's neck, urging him on. I wasn't using a whip.

We came in for the first exchange around twenty-five to thirty miles per hour. I spied Orson, my mugger, holding Blake and waiting for me to dismount in front of the grandstands. Lots of action at the exchange site. Anpo was still running when I leaped from his back and mounted Blake and continued on down the track. I hoped Orson caught Anpo; if not, we would be disqualified.

Five teams were still in the race: Dancing Road, Rising Voice, Medicine Butte, Crow Hop, and Iron Nation. Drums beat loudly, and the crowd cheered us on. Two horses from Cherry Creek and Little River were running around the track, riderless and disqualified.

I kept my focus and urged Blake onward. I was hugging the inside rail on the tepee turn.

Crow Hop came up from behind, passing me, and moved into second place. Then Crow Hop passed Medicine Butte and was in the lead. Dancing Road and Rising Voice trailed behind me. We were coming up on the second exchange.

Orson held the roan stallion and waited for me to ride in. Sun rays reflected off the roan's blue coat. The golden eagle feather tied to his black mane whipped in the wind. With Blake still on the move, I mounted the roan stallion on the run. I barely felt my feet hit the ground. Orson caught Blake. We were still in the game.

Riders from team Dancing Road and Rising Voice failed to mount their horses in the third exchange. Their horses were jumping and rearing from the excitement and noise. Both riders desperately clung to the sides of their horses and tried to mount up. They both failed and ended up facedown in the dirt of the track.

Two more horses were loose on the track and running like they were still in the race. The Dancing Road and Rising Voice teams were disqualified. Their muggers caught the runaway horses and reined them in. The competition grew fierce on the third lap. I trailed behind Crow Hop and Medicine Butte.

The crowd roared as we bore down for the bell lap. This was it.

I whispered medicine to the roan stallion: "Okay, Blue Boy. This is our time. Take us across the finish line just like our dream."

It felt like we were defying gravity. A quarter mile from the finish line, the roan stallion came on strong and passed Crow Hop. We gained on Medicine Butte. Neck and neck, we neared the finish line. I felt one with the roan stallion. My spirit moved into slow motion as we approached the finish line.

Something pulled my eyes toward the grandstands. I couldn't believe it. Standing next to my mother was my father. He was cheering me on. It was true! My dream had come true. Tears flowed like a sacred spring, pure and sweet down my face. The roan passed Medicine Butte and plunged across the finish line. The crowd roared.

A feeling of enlightenment resonated in me, far deeper than anything I'd ever experienced in this world. Iron Nation Relay Team was triumphant. We won the purse and a new tractor for my grandfather. The roan stallion and I did a victory prance in front of the grandstand for good measure. I rode toward the crowd with my eyes focused on my father.

I slid from the roan on the track and gave my friends a big victory hug. I handed the reins to Orson and ran toward my father at the bottom of the bleachers. I silently hugged him for a long time. What could possibly be said to convey what I felt at that moment?

My father wiped the tears from his eyes. "Son, I thought I'd never see you again. You've grown up on me. I'm so proud of you."

I nodded and turned around when Sage gave me a big hug.

She said, "Alfred, you and the roan did it. You won!"

"No," I said, "this was a team effort. We all won!"

Turning to Karl Looking Rock, I thanked him for all his help. I introduced him to my father, and I was surprised to find out they already knew each other.

My father said, "Thank you, Karl, for taking good care of my son. I am forever grateful to you."

Karl replied, "Thank you for your kind words, Elmer Sr., but it was Alfred who took care of me. It's a long story."

They walked toward the sale barn and disappeared into a wave of people. I was sure my father would get an earful of stories.

After all the excitement calmed down, Grandfather stepped forward and said, "You kids go have some fun. Jay and I will take care of your horses. You earned it."

Orson, Sage, Junior, and I walked toward the carnival still in a daze. After a tour of the carnival, I wanted to go for an airplane ride. Sam Winter, who owned the plane, told us he was visiting Karl Looking Rock. They had served in the military together. Sam let us ride for free. It was breathtaking to see the rolling plains below. I imagined the days when herds of buffalo roamed the land like thousands of black dots scattered across the prairie. I was sold. I knew I would be a pilot someday.

We caravanned home, the team in Karl's truck following my parents and Elmer in our Model A Ford, and my grandparents riding with Uncle Jay in his Chevy truck.

On the way home, Karl stopped at Mark Schneider's farm. He lived next to the main road. I hopped out with a pocket full of money and walked up the path toward his front door. I returned to the truck with a big smile on my face. The dream of a tractor for my grandfather had come true.

A New Dawn

We drove on to Beaver Creek to return the roan stallion to his band. As soon as I dropped the ramp of the trailer, the roan ran right toward his waiting band and bucked in a circle.

I shouted out to him, "I love you, Blue Boy! Don't forget about me! I'll be back soon, I promise!"

Sage was excited. She pointed toward the creek and said, "Look over there, a baby foal."

I couldn't believe it. Sure enough, a baby blue roan foal stood next to his mother. I was sure it belonged to the roan stallion.

Karl chuckled. "Well, look at that. We really have a celebration due now. Another champion is born."

Karl drove us back to Iron Nation. On the way home, we decided to keep practicing and try for the next horse relay race coming up in Fort Pierre in two weeks. It was a done deal!

Karl let Orson, Sage, Junior, and their horses off at the Y. They all lived within walking distance. He drove on toward my grandparents' farm. We passed by my parents' two-story frame house that had sat vacant and boarded up for almost two years. I had a gut feeling that old abandoned house would soon be filled with laughter and good times again.

Chepa met me at the gate. He was licking my hands and jumping all over me. I couldn't blame him. I'd missed him too.

Karl helped me unload Anpo. I thanked him again for helping us. He accepted all my compliments like a true Lakota man and teasingly said, "Aww shucks, I could think of a dozen ways you could repay me, like cleaning saddles and . . ."

We both laughed, but I did tell him I would show up next week to help at the ranch. I was sure he just wanted some company.

After watering and feeding Anpo, I put him out to pasture. He loved his freedom and ran in circles, bucking and snorting. Chepa was elated I was home. He darted back and forth in front of me, barking and nipping at my heels. I rubbed him behind his ears to let him know he was still my best friend.

I met my grandfather halfway down the front path. The rumble of wheels on the dry, dust-caked road caught our attention. A farm truck pulled up in the front yard, pulling a skid with a new red tractor tied down on top. It was Mr. Schneider.

With a puzzled look on his face, Grandfather said, "I wonder if he's lost."

"No, he is not lost, Grandfather," I said. "He is delivering your tractor. The tractor I bought for you with the relay money I won." I smiled. "Now you won't have to work so hard."

My grandfather's eyes welled up with tears. He was speechless.

Mr. Schneider leaned his head out the window and said, "Good day, Tom. How've you been? Where do you want your tractor?"

I let the two of them visit, and I headed toward the cabin. I couldn't wait to hear more about my father's long journey home.

I practically skipped up the path. My head filled with all the things I wanted to do and the places I wanted to see. After the airplane ride at White River, I'd decided I was going to be a pilot, as well as an artist, a relay rider, and then again, just me, on a road to another big adventure!

lfreda Beartrack-Algeo is a storyteller and poet as well as an artist and illustrator. She is a member of the Lower Brule Lakota Nation, Kul Wicasa Oyate, Lower Brule, South Dakota, where she grew up surrounded by her extended family, her circle of family and friends. Alfreda uses various art forms to tell her stories. Alfreda says, "It is a very sensitive and beautiful experience to be a storyteller. There is a story in everything I create, from the smallest rock to the mightiest mountain. With every character born, every story shared, I add a piece of my spirit to this great matrix of life. As long as I have a story left to tell, I feel I have a responsibility to gift that story forward." Alfreda currently lives in beautiful Palisade, Colorado, with her spouse, David Algeo.

Look for *River Run*

the exciting conclusion to The Legend of Big Heart *series!*

River Run, the final book in the Big Heart Series, takes place in 1931, during the Great Depression. Teenager Alfred Swallow is forced to attend a cruel Indian boarding school that aims to erase his Lakota identity. To endure the school's harsh rules and conditions, Alfred secretly draws strength from his Native traditions, but the dreadful environment quickly becomes intolerable. One evening, Alfred and his friends escape and run toward freedom, arriving at a nearby river. There, Alfred encounters a carnival caller who immerses him in a world of illusion and magic. Gradually, the carnival members come to accept Alfred, and he comes to love them as family, until he discovers that they have positioned him as the main carnival attraction in a boxing match. Having to rely on his skills, common sense, and instincts, Alfred rapidly learns to trust himself, and in time he becomes the man he was meant to be: Alfred "Big Heart" Swallow.

PathFinders novels offer exciting contemporary and historical stories featuring Native teens and written by Native authors. For more information, visit us at NativeVoicesBooks.com.

Available from your local bookstore or directly from BPC
PO Box 99 • Summertown, TN 38483 • 888-260-8458
Free shipping and handling on all book orders